DEPOSITION
and a
DARE

EVELYN ADAMS

Saints & Sinners

DEPOSITION AND A DARE
A Contemporary Romance
Book One of the Saints and Sinners Series
by
Evelyn Adams
ISBN: 978-1-944801-20-5
Copyright 2017 Evelyn Adams
All rights reserved

Praise for New York Times bestselling author

Evelyn Adams

"Hot, fast, intrigue"

"I want to have dinner with the Southerlands."

"Addictive"

"Scorching hot with heroes to die for and kickass heroines, all wrapped in Southern flair"

"The chemistry is hotter than HOT!"

"Crazy roller coaster love"

"Sexy and smart! Sweet romance, sexy times, and just enough suspense to make this a page turner."

More Books by Evelyn Adams

The Southerland Series
Feel Like Home (Jude and Autumn)
Loving Bailey (Bailey and Trace)
Feels Like Family (Jude and Autumn's Wedding Novella)
Practical Arrangement (Travis and Summer)
Riding the Pause (Rachel and Ian)
A Little Bit Closer (Blake and Samantha)
Love at the Lost & Found (Taylor and Matthew)
Laws of Attraction (Andrew and Candace)
House on Fire (Jake and Genevieve)
Someone to Love (Adam and Erica)
Halfway to Happily Ever After (Taylor and Matt Novella)

Southerland Security Series
Falling Free (Amanda and Michael)
Wicked Intent (Gabe and Berlin)
Closer This Time (Liam and Andy)

Studio 1247 Erotic Romance Series
Love Unbound
Bound to Please
Bound With Love

For the Billionaires Pleasure
Luke & Claire
Wired
Wanton
Won
Wanted
Eric & Julie
Wrapped Around You

For Mallory, thanks for helping me find my way back when I come unmoored and for sharing New Orleans with me.

1

Alex

THE SOFT SWISH OF THE leather flogger cut through the air and I blew out a bored breath, ruffling the few wisps of hair that slipped from my braided ponytail. Arching my back for effect, I tugged gently at the padded leather cuffs, being careful not to pull free. The bite of the rough wood against my mostly bare ass helped wake me up as I counted down the minutes until the appointment was over.

Peter, the hundred-and-sixty-pound accountant in pleather pants, winced as he worked me over with the flogger. I'm using *worked over* in the most generous way possible. In reality, I was unlikely to feel either pleasure or pain from poor Peter's ministrations. The only real danger was being tickled to death while he tried to channel his inner Dom, visibly cringing every time the leather hit my flesh.

"Is it okay, Lexi?" A bead of sweat caused by nerves, not exertion, clung to his upper lip.

Here's where it got tricky. The whole consent/non-consent issue. The men who hired me were looking for a practice submissive. Someone discreet who could help them work out their moves before they take them out to the real world. Sex was on a case-by-case basis. Not that that particular case had come up yet, but I was keeping my options open. Nudity was a given.

Peter's CEO girlfriend would probably rather he didn't look at my naked tits, but honest to God, I had to figure out a way to keep the man motivated. The flogger didn't do it for him, but my tits kept him in the game. I doubted his girlfriend, I think her name was Sarah, would ever know about me, but if I managed to teach Peter how to take charge in the bedroom, she'd be grateful for my help, nipples and all.

"We talked about this, remember?" I gently admonished the timid man. The last thing I wanted to do was make him more uncertain. I'd be stuck on the cross forever. "You don't ask; you tell. You watch your partner's reaction to what you're doing, and then you decide when she's had enough. If you're concerned, remind her to use her safe word. Do not ask her if what you're doing is okay. You're the one in charge."

He nodded, but I could tell by the way his Adam's apple bobbed when he swallowed that he still wasn't comfortable with the idea.

"Go ahead and try again. This time put your back into it."

I arched, pressing my tits toward him, and waited to feel something—anything—as the flogger came down again.

It took him two or three tries, but he finally hit his stride, and by the time the session ended, he'd managed to shed some of his inhibitions. He was unlikely to rock Sarah's world, but I was pretty sure he could manage a decent rumble. If he did, he might become a repeat client.

"Remember the aftercare," I said as a clearly pleased with himself Peter unfastened the cuff around my right wrist. "We won't practice it, but with the woman you're dominating, you're going to need to hold her and reassure her. Make her feel safe and cherished when you're done playing."

Peter wasn't going to need help with the aftercare. The hard part for him would be not apologizing. He nodded, reaching for the cuff around my left wrist. Now that we'd finished, he seemed to be in as much of a hurry to leave as me. He left me to unfasten the cuffs around my ankles, and by the time I stepped away from the St. Andrew's Cross, he was headed for the door. I expected as much. Once I was freed from my bonds, I was a naked woman and not someone he wanted to remember he'd paid to help him.

"She's going to be amazed," I called after him as he slipped on his coat and yanked open the door. I shimmied into my bra in time to see another man slip through the doorway and past a horrified-looking Peter, who either assumed I knew the guy or was too chicken-shit to stick around.

I didn't know the guy. I'd put a fairly elaborate screening process in place to weed out the assholes just looking for someone to smack around, and honestly, it almost never came up. The building that housed my studio was secure, which didn't explain why there was a hipster, rocking a man bun and carrying a beat-up messenger bag, standing in the doorway and paying particular attention to my G-string and mostly bare breasts.

"What the fuck are you doing here?" I asked, drawing his gaze from my tits to my face.

He held the folded legal-looking piece of paper out in front of him, his eyebrows arched in clear approval.

"Alexandra Smithson," he said as I reach for the paper. "You've been served."

I STILL HAD the folded paper clutched in my sweaty hand when the cab stopped in front of the bar. I was late and dashed for the front door, stumbling when my five-inch-high fuck-me heels caught on a crack in the pavement. I would have landed on my knees, but a strong, firm arm reached out and snagged me around the waist before I went down. He didn't so much steady me as set me back on my feet. As soon as I was sure my heels would hold me, I looked up into the eyes of my rescuer. Whiskey-colored eyes with bronze flecks, the kind that went dark chocolate when the owner really wanted something. Forcing myself to breathe and to stop thinking stupid shit about wanting, I managed a smile.

"Thanks," I said to the man who'd saved my knees and my pride.

The cut of his suit made it clear he didn't buy his clothes off the rack, and his dark-brown hair curled over his collar in a way that would have looked feminine on a different man. On him, it added to the barely civilized pirate vibe. But it was his lips that kept pulling at my attention. Soft, warm, full lips, curved in a smile that said he knew more than anyone else around him and was enjoying the joke.

"I assure you; the pleasure is mine," he said, managing to make it sound like he'd done more than catch me.

I nodded and pulled away, trying not to show my surprise when he held the door open and followed me into the dimly lit room. I felt him behind me, a warm presence at my back in the crush of people jockeying for space at the bar. Forcing my attention away from the man I was sure I was safer not knowing, I squinted as my eyes adjusted. I scanned the tables around the bar for my friends, and by the time I found the women who were closer to me than family, Mr. Tall, Dark, and Dangerous had disappeared into the crowd.

"Finally," said Meredith. "Did you get tied up with a client?" The freckles over the bridge of her nose crinkled as she grinned at her own play on words. I knew she hated the tiny spots that dotted her pale Irish-cream complexion, but along with the red hair and emerald eyes, she was fresh-faced and stunning, more suited to windswept moors than grubby city streets. She was also a hopeless romantic, a tendency she'd thankfully been able to channel into her wedding cake bakery, I Dough.

"Funny," I said. "This is why I'm late." I slapped the paper on the table. "I got served, and please spare me the puns this time." I held up my hand, but I didn't need to. Something in my tone must have betrayed the slight edge of hysteria I'd been feeling since the smug ogling man handed me the summons.

Charlotte reached for the paper, scanning it quickly in the dim light of the bar. "Okay, it's not Armageddon," she said, glancing up from under her inky lashes.

With her glossy blonde hair and doe eyes I can only mimic with an abundance of makeup, Charlotte could easily be mistaken for a sexy Alice in Wonderland. It was a misconception she'd put to good use for her clients. The opposing counsel almost always underestimated her until they got their shirts handed to them. It had earned her the nickname Tiger Shark with the other lawyers who had gone up against her. She was beautiful, deadly, and her attacks came when you least expected them. I was glad she was on my side.

"It feels like the end of the world," I said, but my chest relaxed a fraction of an inch. Exhaling, I collapsed into a vacant seat next to Elena.

"I know," said Charlotte. "Legal stuff always does, but don't worry. I can refer you to someone who handles these kinds of cases all the time. He owes me."

Her eyes narrowed and just like that, the shark replaced the wide-eyed innocent. I could only imagine why he owed her, but I had no doubt Charlotte could make him pay up.

"Can't you do it? I'd feel so much better if you were handling it."

"Handling what?" asked Kindra, pressing her cheek to mine before sliding into the chair next to me. The spicy floral scent of her perfume managed to be exotic and familiar at the same time.

"A film company filed a cease-and-desist against Alex and the Gentleman's Submissive."

"Do they have a case?" asked Kindra before turning her warm brown eyes on me. Her sympathetic gaze was reassuring. She always seemed to know exactly how to do that, which was part of what made her such a damn fine psychiatrist, but right now I wanted Charlotte's reassurance that I wasn't going to lose everything I'd worked so hard to build.

When I graduated with a masters in psychology and a PhD in genders studies and no prospects other than sales clerk at the soon-to-be out-of-business indie bookstore, I had to make a career for myself. I wanted to teach, or rather I wanted to write a book that would change the world—kind of a *Men are from Mars; Women are from Venus* for smart women and the enlightened men who loved them. Being a professor seemed like the best way to get there. Except there were only a couple of dozen jobs in my chosen field, and they were all currently occupied by other people. The obscure degree from the well-known university let me move in better social circles, but it didn't offer anything else except astronomical student loans, which I now had to pay back.

So, I took what I learned from contemporary women's fiction, and I started the Gentleman's Submissive. It seemed pretty obvious to me with the popularity of BDSM-lite books and movies that women were interested in the fantasy of being dominated by a strong male. Nothing new, I know, but given how much we'd heaped on our plates in the last three or four decades, the desire seemed stronger than ever. Equally obvious was the fact that very few men had any idea what a Dom did, let alone how to become one for his partner.

That's where I stepped in, wearing my G-string and stilettos. I have no illusions about training real Doms. I'm not sure they exist—not in the classic definition anyway. What I do is try to give men like Peter the confidence they need to give their partner some of what they want. No easy feat, let me tell you, especially with men as tentative (read clueless) as most of the men who come to me.

"It's too soon to tell, but even if they have a case, it doesn't mean they'll win." She reached across the table for my hand. "Or even that the case will ever make it to court. In fact, it's odd that they'd jump to filing a complaint so quickly. Usually there would be a lot more back-and-forth before it got to this point. Most of these kinds of suits are about settling, not going to trial."

My hand clenched involuntarily at the mention of court. I'd never dealt with more than an unpaid parking ticket. The idea of going to court scared the crap out of me.

"It's okay, baby. The guy I know is a lousy lay but a phenomenal intellectual property attorney. I'm sure he can make this go away, and if not, he's more than up for a fight."

"Can't you handle it?" I repeated, hating the slight whine in my voice but too worried to do much about it.

"I specialize in cheating husbands, not copyright issues. Waters knows more about it than I do. Really, Alex, you'd be in better hands with him."

"I don't care. I trust you."

"Can't you do it?" asked Meredith, turning her green eyes on Charlotte. "You put the fear of God into millionaires and their attorneys on a regular basis. How hard could it be to get a movie producer to back down?"

"She has a point," said Elena.

I plastered my best *you know you wanna help me* look on my face and hoped we'd managed to wear Charlotte down.

"Fine," she finally said, rolling her eyes. "I still think you'd be better off with Waters but I'll at least start the process. But…" She held up her index finger when I started to squeal. "If I ever feel like I'm jeopardizing your chances, I'm getting out. No argument."

"Deal," I said, jumping up to reach across the table to hug her. "Thank you so much."

"Don't thank me until it's over. I might fuck it up." Charlotte gave her head a shake but I could tell by the way her lips curved that she wasn't as concerned as her words sounded.

"You won't," I said, knowing it was true. The women at the table loved me. Any one of them would do whatever it took to make things right, and I'd do the same for them.

"I wish I had your confidence. I feel like I'm swimming upstream right now." She took a sip of her wine and a wrinkle creased her forehead. I'd been so absorbed—understandably maybe, but still—in my own stuff, I hadn't noticed Charlotte's expression.

"With work or something else?" asked Kindra, scooting her chair closer.

"I have a client. He's a friend, or he was," said Charlotte, looking almost uncertain. "His wife says he cheated on her, and she's filed for divorce. He asked me to represent him."

"You're defending a cheater?" asked Meredith, her eyes wide enough to see white around the green.

Her disbelief was understandable. Of all of us, Charlotte seemed to have the fewest rules but as far as I knew, she'd never represented someone who'd cheated. She'd made an impressive living taking the adulterers to the cleaners. It was a point of personal pride.

"Do you think he did it?" asked Kindra.

"I don't know. I always liked him. He was a dog in college, but he was honest about it. You knew what you were getting," she said, her lips curving at the memory. "Looking in from the outside, how can you really know what someone's like?"

That was true, I thought, nodding. I'd done a couple of sessions with a ball-busting corporate trader who took companies apart for fun. At first glance, he looked like an alpha on steroids, but not only did he have trouble being dominant sexually, by the end of our first session, I wondered if he'd be happier if we switched places. He seemed so uncomfortable even role-playing when I suggested it to him. It was the last time I saw him.

"True, but what do you think?" asked Kindra, sliding seamlessly into her professional persona.

"He swears he didn't do it." Charlotte rolled her eyes at the disbelieving looks around the table. It wasn't that any of us hated men, but none of us were the naïve girls we'd started out as. "I know. I know," she said, holding her hands up in front of her. "I have a hard time believing it too, but he signed a prenup giving her half of everything if he cheats. I can't see him risking the company he built from the ground up just to get his dick sucked."

I fought the urge to roll my eyes and kept my gaze fixed to hers. I've known men who'd risked a lot more to get off.

"Admittedly, it's a long shot," said Charlotte. "But it's not fair for him to lose what he's worked so hard for if he didn't do it."

"You like him," said Meredith, at the same time Kindra said, "You believe him."

"I'm not sure," said Charlotte, looking miserable. "And what's worse, I can't trust that one thing isn't feeding the other."

She wouldn't be the first woman to make a stupid choice about a man for what seemed like a rational reason, I thought. I let my eyes drift over my friend's shoulder, remembering a list of stupid choices I've made. My gaze landed on Mr. Tall, Dark, and Dangerous, watching me from a group of men gathered near the bar.

Perfect case in point.

I looked away, feeling my face flush, wondering why simply meeting his eyes would make me blush. I was long past the age when a man's attention made me self-conscious.

"Can you get him out of the prenup?" I asked, dragging my attention back to the conversation in front of me.

"I can try, but it looks ironclad, even for me," said Charlotte, a fierce glint in her eyes. "I'd feel better if I had something on her or an alibi from him. Or even knew exactly what she had on him. I'll figure something out."

She sounded determined, which was something. I had a feeling a determined Charlotte could move mountains.

"Enough of legal stuff," she said, her clear blue gaze meeting mine, wordlessly willing me to relax. "What's going on with the rest of you?"

I laughed with the others as Meredith told a story about a bride who wanted a penguin wedding cake. When the waiter brought our drinks, I glanced at the doorway, not sure whether to be relieved or disappointed to find Mr. Tall, Dark, and Dangerous gone.

ERIK

"TOOK YOU LONG enough." Jared slapped me on the back and put a rocks glass of Macallan in my hand. There was an advantage to having friends who knew me so well.

"I got sidetracked on the way in." I took a swallow of the smoky amber liquid, remembering how fucking good the petite detour with the big eyes and tight curves felt in my arms.

I glanced in the direction she'd gone when we parted and found her sitting at a table with a group of women. Her face turned in my direction as if she'd felt my gaze, and I sucked in a breath at the sucker punch to my gut when her eyes met mine. If the speed with which she glanced away was any indication, she'd felt it too.

"Nice," said Ben, stretching his neck to follow the direction of my gaze. "It's about time you got interested in someone. Which one was she?"

"The redhead is stunning," said Jared. "Hell, they all are. Want to move the party over there?"

Actually, friends might be overrated, I thought, uncertain why the idea of reducing the encounter to a pickup opportunity bothered me.

"Matt's waiting for us in the kitchen. He's going to be pissed if we ruin his oysters." The excuse sounded lame, but it's all I had.

"You sure, man? It's been a long time since Julie," said Ben, his voice taking on a serious note that wouldn't get us anywhere I wanted to be.

"Positive. Let's go before Chef has an aneurysm." I tossed back the last of my Scotch and turned toward the door to the kitchen, not waiting to see if the others followed me. The sooner I got the beautiful woman who managed to bring all my protective instincts roaring to life out of my sight, the sooner I'd be able to get her out of my mind.

Matt was cursing up a blue streak behind the line. Not at his staff. I'd known the temperamental chef long enough to know he was a ball buster, but he didn't fit the *terrifying the line cooks* stereotype, especially since so many of them were older than him. He made it a point to hire people with roots in Creole cooking and then help refine what they already knew. If he'd had to swear at them, they'd have been gone already.

From the sound of it, some poor patron had the nerve to order the trout amandine without the almonds and with the meunière sauce on the side. Matt was worse than Frank Lloyd Wright in his obsession to details. Wright built in furniture so his clients wouldn't mess up his designs by moving in their own things. Matt gave people his food the way they were supposed to eat it.

"It's not trout amandine without the almonds. May as well make it without the fucking fish. *Cochons.*"

By the expression on their faces, a couple of the cooks might have sympathy for the patron with the possible nut allergy, but they weren't about to say it out loud.

"Pesky customers getting in the way of your genius again?" I asked, moving close enough to the line so Matt could see me but not close enough to get in the way of the white-jacketed servers hurrying to pick up finished plates.

If the restaurant's dining room and bar with its white tablecloth tables and bottle-lined walls were an homage to Tennessee Williams's New Orleans, the kitchen belonged to Degas. It was copper vent hoods and scarred wooden counters and the heady aroma of charbroiled meat and peppers—fire to the cool civility of the front of the house scene.

"About fucking time," said Matt, glancing up from the fish he was preparing. "Go sit down." He motioned with his head to the chef's table tucked in one corner of the kitchen. He occasionally did VIP dinners for patrons who wanted a more intimate experience, but not as often as he could have. Mainly, I guessed, because he couldn't hold his tongue.

"The hospitality is inspirational, man," said Jared.

"Fuck you." Ignoring us, he turned and gave a few brief instructions to the cook beside him before picking up a platter from the cold prep part of the line and coming around the counter to meet us. "Nina," he said, grabbing a server as she went past. "Get someone to bring us a bottle of the Trevisiol."

"Yes, Chef," she said, changing directions to hurry off and do his bidding.

"Eat them before the ice melts." He set the platter of oysters on the well-worn wooden table in front of us and watched while I lifted one of the shells from its bed of crushed ice.

I brought the oyster to my lips and tipped the entire thing into my mouth, not bothering to stifle my groan of pleasure as the sweet briney liquor hit the back of my palate.

"What is that?" I liked my oysters with cocktail sauce I knew better than to ask for, but what Matt offered us was something so much better. There was the clean taste of icy-fresh oyster combined with the sharp bite of citrus, topped with a heat that was more than simple pepper.

"Gulf oysters with kumquat and pink peppercorn granita," said Matt. He picked up a shell and tossed back an oyster, smiling like someone immensely pleased with himself. "They go on the menu this weekend."

We made quick work of the rest of the oysters while Nina returned with a bottle of prosecco and four stemless flutes. The crisp sparkling wine was perfect with the mineral taste of the oysters. I resisted the urge to wax on about the pairing. No reason for Matt's head to get any bigger. He knew he was a master; reinforcing it just made him harder to live with.

He motioned to the older man expediting and four plates appeared, holding chunks of seared mustard crusted beef on a bed of white beans. Matt hadn't bothered to ask how we wanted our steak cooked. I honestly don't think he cared, which worked for me, I thought as I cut into the perfectly rare filet.

"Are you playing this weekend?" asked Ben after Nina cleared our plates and swapped our wine glasses for rocks glasses of Scotch.

I took a swallow of the Macallan, letting the earthy amber liquid roll around on my tongue while I waited for somebody else to answer. Since Julie left, I didn't play as much as the others. I didn't want to. Or I hadn't until an hour or so earlier when the beautiful brunette fell into my arms, which was crazy. I wasn't interested in anything serious. Fun maybe, but nothing that even whispered at a relationship. Ending things with Julie cured me of those impulses.

I'd never seen the woman before, which meant she probably wasn't already in the lifestyle. It was a small enough community and I'd remember those big brown eyes. I loved the way her clothes screamed sex, but she still blushed for me. Her hesitation to meet my gaze and the way she'd softened in my arms made me think there was more there. Much more, but that could be my protective side. Seeing her almost fall and then catching her pushed every one of my buttons. Closet submissive or not, it didn't matter. I wasn't interested in being part of anyone's BDSM Welcome Wagon.

"Maybe you can bring the woman who sidetracked you to the club," said Jared.

It took me a moment to realize he was talking to me, and I shook myself back to the present.

"You hardly ever play anymore," said Matt. "Not since she-who-must-not-be-named."

Ben snorted. "He made a Harry Potter kink reference. That's all kinds of fucked up."

"I'm not wrong," said Matt, his expression uncharacteristically sympathetic, which only set my nerves even more on edge. "It's time for you to get back in the game. Someone new could be good for you."

I hadn't been to Bacchus since the clusterfuck—not the fun kind, either—months ago. I could still picture the expression on the guy's face as the bouncers dragged him out of the club after he went too far with the woman he had bound to the horse. He'd kept insisting he'd known what he was doing. That he'd been trained. It seemed like every heterosexual guy in the world was turning into a self-proclaimed Dom and none of them knew what they were doing. I couldn't do much about the glut of Dom wannabes, but I sure as hell intended to do everything in my power to make sure no one else got hurt. That was as far as my involvement in the club was going to go.

"I'm not interested in anything aside from this twenty-five-year-old single malt," I said, determined to steer the conversation in a different direction.

I tried to call Julie's face to mind to help me remember why jumping into something new was a bad idea. But instead of blonde hair and blue eyes, my mind filled with dark hair and brown ones.

Alex

"EXPLAIN TO ME AGAIN WHAT we're doing here." I smoothed the skirt of my ladies who lunch suit and snagged a mimosa I was sure was more carb-laden orange juice than champagne from the tray of a passing waiter.

"I'm here to make nice with future clients, and you're here because you love me, and you don't have anything better to do." Elena hit me with a smile that dared me to contradict her, her hazel eyes lighting up mischievously.

She'd pulled her light-brown hair back into a smooth twist and she wore the Chanel suit like she'd been born for it. I knew better. She'd been raised by a single mother in a house it would be generous to call modest. The veneer of wealth she wore like a second skin was earned, not her birthright. She'd paid for it by having exquisite taste and the ability to transform a space into something both beautiful and uniquely suited to its inhabitants. She might not have the pull or the client lists of some of the older, more established interior design firms yet, but she would. With her drive and skill, I didn't have any doubts that it was only a matter of time before she ruled the city.

"I have lots of things to do." She arched an elegantly groomed eyebrow at me and I didn't bother trying to hide my smirk. "Okay, maybe not, but I do love you."

It was odd not to have to go to work every day. I'd gotten used to logging in a generous number of client hours every week, but my business was more than that. I spent easily twice as much time on marketing and coaxing potential clients to take the plunge and hire me. Glancing around the room at the polished to within an inch of their lives women, I wondered if any of them had benefited from my services. I hoped so. Every woman deserved her orgasms the way she wanted them, but with the cease-and-desist hanging over my head, it was hard to think of any of that.

"So what do we do?" I might not be able to think about my own business, but I could at least help my friend. "Divide and conquer? Thin the weak from the herd?"

"Sure. Nothing says high-end interior design like hunting metaphors." Elena set her half-empty glass on the nearby tray. She clearly exercised more restraint when it came to carbs than I did. "Just be nice. Charming, if you can manage it without hurting yourself. Being seen at these things gives me credibility when I'm asking people to trust me with their homes. They feel more comfortable if someone they know recommends me or they recognize me from one of these things. Until I score a big job like something on the Garden District Home Tour, this is my best advertising."

It made sense and despite my current emotional state, I ought to be able to manage friendly and approachable, if not charming. I followed Elena to a table with two empty chairs and shared smiles with the women already seated. My friend quickly fell into a conversation with the woman sitting next to her. It wasn't exactly a *what do you do for a living* kind of crowd and I searched my brain for an opening line. Thankfully, I was saved by a size-zero blonde in a simple sheath dress I was sure cost more than most people's mortgage payments, tapping on the open mic.

"Hello," she said with a nervous giggle as the mic amplified her voice. "I'd like to thank you all for coming today to support such a noble cause. Before we get started with the rest of the program, I'd like to introduce one of our most important benefactors, Counselor Erik Jensen."

I glanced from the mimosa I was sucking down to the head table to see who was the unlucky dude in a room full of bored rich wives, and the breath caught in my throat.

Mr. Tall, Dark, and Dangerous was making his way to the microphone. Good Lord, my memory hadn't done him justice. If anything, he was more delicious than I remembered. His custom-made suit—the man had seriously fine taste in clothes—was charcoal this time, with a scarlet silk tie I was trying not to picture wrapped around my fist. Or tied around my wrists. When he stretched out his arms to grab the podium, I got a glimpse of tanned wrists and small onyx cufflinks.

For someone who made a living from others' fetishes, I had remarkably few of my own, but if I had to name one, it was a man's wrists. I loved how strong they were, how different from mine, how they looked against my pale skin. Add a good watch and I'd go weak in the knees. Mr. Tall, Dark, and Dangerous was wearing a very good watch.

I had to stop thinking of him like that. I had a name for him now. *Erik Jensen.* And then he opened his mouth and my good intentions died.

"Domestic violence is an important cause to me, perhaps the most important," he said, his melted caramel voice washing over the room. "There are few sins a man can commit worse than mistreating a woman or child. I'm grateful to be able to support an organization that works so hard to protect the women of this city and their families. Thank you for having me and thank you for the work you do."

Unless you were talking about signing a check, I doubted that any of the women in the room did any actual work. That didn't stop them from applauding loudly at Mr. Jensen's compliment. They were still clapping as he made his way from the podium and out the door. The disappointment in the room was palpable when the other women realized he wasn't coming back, but for me, it was the first time I could catch my breath since he'd taken the stage.

He hadn't noticed me. There was no reason for him to recognize me. I was sure he'd made more of an impression on me than I had him. That didn't stop my heart from trying to double time its way out of my chest. *What was wrong with me?* I spent my days with men, being tied up by men. I thought I was long past the point when a simple attraction could knock me off my game. There was something about this man, something I couldn't put a name to that was different from all the others.

With an increasingly familiar mixture of regret and relief, I turned my attention back to making conversation with the woman on my right.

"YOU'RE AWFULLY DRESSED up," said Charlotte hours later, tapping her pale-pink lacquered nail against her desk.

I hadn't bothered to go home to change after the benefit. Although after the overworked chicken mousse quenelles and baby vegetables, I'd been tempted to go for second lunch. In a city known for its food, it had been a disappointment, definitely not worth the calories I'd have to burn off later, which wouldn't have stopped me if Elena had been willing to grab a po' boy or beans and rice somewhere. But if we'd done that, I'd have told her about meeting Erik Jensen—if I could even call it that—and I wasn't ready to do that. I didn't like how unsettled he made me feel, and I didn't want to try to explain it to anyone. At least not yet.

"I had a *ladies who lunch* thing with Elena. You said you had news?" *Please let it be that all of this was a big mistake and I could get on with my life.* I'd been playing every possible doomsday scenario in my head since I got Charlotte's message. Dropping to the couch, I held my breath and waited for my friend to tell me everything was going to be okay.

She leaned forward in her chair, and my pulse kicked up about a hundred notches. "Our motion to dismiss was denied. I expected it to be." She hurried on before I had a chance to swallow my tongue. "We didn't really have any grounds to dismiss, but I had to try anyway. It would've been foolish not to."

"So what happens now?" I asked, sucking in a breath and trying to get my racing heart to slow the fuck down.

"The court has scheduled the case management conference for Monday. After that, we'll have a better idea of what to expect. The big thing right now is to keep them from being able to subpoena your client records."

She may have said more but I couldn't hear over the ringing in my ears. If they were able to get the names of my clients, it wouldn't matter what happened with the lawsuit. I'd be out of business before it ever went to trial. Discretion was essential to my work.

"Hey, don't worry," said Charlotte, coming out from behind her desk to sit on the couch with me. "I won't let that happen. Things are moving faster than they usually do. I'm not sure why but it's not a bad thing. And regardless of what the other party wants, the court wants us to settle."

I didn't know whether to find that reassuring or not. I wasn't sure what settling would mean. I'd managed to squirrel a small amount of money away in savings, but if I had to change the name of my company or my brand, it would be like starting over from scratch. Worse. No one would take a chance on me if they had any inkling their identity might be exposed.

"What time on Monday? What do I need to bring?" I asked when I could breathe again.

"Nothing. You don't need to be there. I can handle it myself."

"I want to be there." I couldn't imagine sitting at home waiting to find out what was going to happen to my future.

"They won't let you in the room," said Charlotte. "The CMC is between counsel and the court. It's just to set the schedule for discovery, any expert witnesses, and a trial date."

When she said trial date, the ringing started in my ears again. I must not have done a very good job of hiding my fear, because she reached for my hand.

"It's okay, Alex. I promise. It'll be okay," she said, giving my hand a reassuring squeeze. "You can come if you want to, but you'll have to wait outside the room."

"I can do that." I nodded, wondering how I was supposed to sit in the hallway and wait for someone else to decide what was going to happen to the business I'd worked so hard to build.

ERIK

I GLANCED AT my watch and told myself for the tenth time to get a grip on my fucking emotions. Thinking and feeling rarely went hand-in-hand, and thinking was what I needed for this case. Letting my emotions drive wasn't normally a problem for me. In the eight years I'd been practicing law, I hadn't come across a case that yanked my chain as badly as this one. Back Door Cinema versus Alexandra Smithson hit a little too close to home.

After the debacle at Bacchus, I'd gone looking for the Lexi the asshole wannabe said *trained* him. I might have embellished my role at the club to convince him I held his fate in my hands, but I had no problem getting him to turn over the contact information for the Gentleman's Submissive. Hell, by the time I finished, he'd have turned over his mother to avoid having what happened at the club go public.

A bit of digging online led me to Back Door Cinema and their Gentleman's Submissive film collection. Once they realized I was going to get them money and it wouldn't cost them anything upfront, they jumped at the chance to become my new client. By the time I finished talking, the film company owner actually seemed to believe a professional submissive on the other side of the state had wronged the adult entertainment company he ran out of his garage. It took some legal massaging to justify the cease-and-desist, but I managed it.

The Gentleman's Submissive website was fairly vague. Given the nature of the business, I hadn't expected to find much information online and under normal circumstances, it probably wouldn't be enough to prevail in this kind of suit. I was motivated. I was tired of seeing people playing pretend at something that was part of who I am. I doubted that Lexi, as her clients called her, had ever been to a dungeon or submitted to a real Dom. I pictured her as a spoiled girl wearing leather and playing around with something she didn't understand.

Even that wouldn't have mattered. Everyone should get to explore their sexuality the way they wanted, even if it meant making an ass of themselves. I was a huge proponent of self-expression. The problem I had was that she thought she could train people to do something she obviously didn't understand, and that was fraud. Her fraud led to someone getting hurt, which was intolerable.

The chamber door opened, and I glanced over my shoulder to see Charlotte Ellis enter. I'd never gone up against the petite blonde before. I hadn't even heard of her until I saw her name on the court papers and did a little research. She usually handled divorce cases, and she had a well-earned reputation for taking powerful men to the cleaners. She looked more like a China doll than a cutthroat attorney, and I didn't doubt many men had made the mistake of underestimating her. I wouldn't, but I still wasn't sure what she was doing handling an intellectual property case. Unless the defendant was a friend of hers, or given her penchant for eating powerful men for lunch and her client's patronizing business model, more likely they were both part of some women's club that hated men.

"Ms. Ellis?" I said, offering her my hand. I knew from the picture on her firm's website who she was, but it never hurt to ask an easy question, and it certainly never hurt to get someone used to saying yes before you asked for what you really wanted.

"Mr. Jensen." She took my hand without so much as a nod of agreement, and there was steel in her clear blue eyes. *No, it wouldn't do to underestimate her.*

I nodded, grinning in spite of myself as a side door opened and the judge and clerk entered the chambers. It was Judge Black, and I clenched my jaw to hide my grimace. The Honorable Judge Black was notorious for pushing for a settlement in civil cases. Regardless of what my client wanted, settling wouldn't suit my purpose this time. I shouldn't even be thinking like that. *Again with the emotions.* Lawyers were supposed to get the best deal he could for their clients and keep their own crap out of it. I couldn't help it. I wasn't going to be satisfied until the Gentleman's Submissive was out of business. I wasn't looking for just a punitive settlement; I wanted her gone.

"Counselors," said the judge. "I assume you have proposed schedules for discovery and some requests for me."

"Yes, Your Honor," said Ms. Ellis. "I have our list of potential witnesses. Because of the nature of Ms. Smithson's business, it would be irreparably damaging to her reputation should her client list be made public, not to mention the potential damage to many others' reputations. Because the names of clients are not directly relevant to this case, I would urge Your Honor to deny any request made by the opposing counsel to subpoena the records."

On the word *urge*, Judge Black arched an eyebrow and gave Ms. Ellis a look that said she'd overplayed her hand. She'd also jumped the gun, and I couldn't help but grin at her obvious discomfort.

"The prosecution will not be asking to subpoena client records. There is no reason for the people who've already paid for Ms. Smithson's *training* to be subjected to even more trouble as a result of Ms. Smithson's questionable business practices."

I was sure I'd caught Ms. Ellis off guard by not requesting a subpoena for the client list, but I wouldn't be part of contributing to an invasion of the so-called clients' privacy if I could help it.

"My client is obviously anxious to move things along as quickly as possible," I said. "Every day the Gentleman's Submissive is allowed to remain in business, it's infringing on the rights of my client."

"I understand your concern, Counselor," said the judge. "But I will not be pushed for a trial date. I *urge*," the judge glanced over at Ms. Ellis, "both parties to make every effort to come to a solution before going to trial."

We bantered back and forth a bit about dates. Since neither party seemed interested in dragging out the process, there was surprisingly little disagreement about the schedule, and in less than half an hour, I was nodding to the judge as he left the chamber and snapping my briefcase closed. I tipped my head to Ms. Ellis, who was still tucking papers away as I made my way out the door. I barely managed to hide the break in my stride when I saw the beautiful young woman waiting on the bench in the hallway.

It was the woman from the bar. The one who'd almost fallen in front of me. The same woman who'd managed to rattle my concentration at the benefit. I'd gotten used to her invading my dreams, but I didn't have any idea what she was doing here, looking like Gal Gadot when Steve Trevor tried to hide her under layers of tweed. The woman in front of me was all wide-eyed innocent and buttoned-up sex in her demure gray suit. Her soft-pink blouse was the only hint at the lush woman underneath the severely cut suit. I knew exactly how fantastic her body was hidden under all that gray. I'd felt it when I held her in my arms.

She stood as if she was there for me, and her gaze met mine. For a moment, it was as if there was some invisible thread tying us together. Some kind of current moving between us, which was fucking rubbish. She was a woman. I wanted her. If the look in her eyes was any indication, she wanted me too. Simple chemistry. It was not some kind of crazy fates colliding situation. The fact that I could still remember how she felt in my arms and that she pulled on every possessive urge I had was incidental.

As I watched, her gaze slid past me and over my shoulder. When I glanced back, Ms. Ellis was hurrying toward us.

"How did it go?" asked the woman I desperately needed to get to know better. Like naked tied to my bed better.

I gave my head a shake to clear away the image of peeling off that gray suit and sliding pink silk over warm flesh until I uncovered the soft, warm woman underneath. *What the fuck was I thinking?* At the very least, she was a close friend of the opposing counsel. Or she might be... *Fuck me. Hard.*

Ms. Ellis shook her head almost imperceptibly and the other woman's eyes went wide, glancing from me to her attorney and back again, obviously coming to the same conclusion that just smacked me in the head.

"Alexandra Smithson," I said, not bothering to phrase the words as a question when I already knew the answer. *Unfucking believable.* The woman who'd been playing a starring role in my dreams at night was the same woman I planned to ruin.

I watched the slender column of her throat—a throat I'd pictured with my hand wrapped gently around it as I surged inside her—move as she swallowed hard.

"Erik Jensen," she said, sounding a little breathless.

I shouldn't like the way my name sounded from her lips, but damn it to hell, I did.

"How do you two know each other?" asked Ms. Ellis, glancing suspiciously from her client to me.

"We bumped into each other in front of a friend's restaurant a few weeks ago, and again more recently at a domestic violence luncheon." I had the pleasure of watching her brown eyes widen when she realized I'd noticed her at the benefit.

It was a short-lived triumph. She straightened, shifting her weight almost imperceptibly, and it was as if she'd slipped on another persona as easily as if she'd put on a coat. She took a deep breath, arching her back slightly and emphasizing her breasts. Without changing one article of clothing, she'd gone from innocent librarian to sex kitten.

The shift reminded me of exactly why we were there. Ms. Smithson used her sexuality for power and money. I'd just have to tell the protective part of me to shut the fuck up because I didn't want anything she was selling. And I damn sure wouldn't let anyone else get caught in her scheme.

"I will see you on the eighth for the start of discovery. I'll allow myself the pleasure of conducting your interrogatory myself, Ms. Smithson." I took a step closer, fully intending to put her off-balance and make her uncomfortable. It worked. She held her own, not giving any ground but her nostrils flared, and I saw her hands clench into fists at her sides. *Good.* I wanted her defensive. It would make my job that much easier. "And then after that," I said, closing the last bit of distance between us, "I'll make sure you stop playing with things you don't understand and taking innocent people along with you."

"That's enough," said Ms. Ellis, physically inserting herself between us.

"Not yet," I said, backing away from the women. "But by the time I'm done, it will be. See you on the eighth, ladies." I saw a flash of fear in Ms. Smithson's dark eyes and had to remind myself of all the trouble she'd caused and the arrogance with which she conducted her business. I couldn't let myself forget or I was afraid I'd do something I might regret. Part of me worried I already had.

3

Alex

I THUMBED THE ANTACID OUT of the top of the quickly diminishing roll as I waited for the receptionist to acknowledge me. Peter—no surprise—hadn't called back for another appointment, and I'd put off the few new inquiries I'd gotten until after the eighth. It didn't matter. My heart wasn't in it. I found it increasingly difficult to think about work with the date for the interrogatories looming. The best I could hope for out of the day was pretty toes.

"Thanks so much for squeezing me in," I said to the receptionist as I bit down on the antacid, chewing discreetly until the fruit taste filled my mouth.

I'd been practically living on the rolls of chalky goodness since my last encounter at the courthouse with Erik Jensen. I couldn't think of him as Mr. Tall, Dark, and Dangerous any more, not when he had so clearly positioned himself in the Dangerous-only category.

"My pleasure," said the receptionist. "Right this way."

She came around the counter and led me toward one of the high leather chairs sitting in a row at the back of the salon.

"Can I get you something to drink? Coffee or champagne?" she asked.

"Champagne would be lovely, thank you." It was barely noon, but nothing went better with antacids than champagne.

A petite Asian woman took the bottle of nail polish I'd chosen and set it on the rolling cart beside her. She placed my feet in the warm scented water, and the receptionist placed a champagne flute in my hand. For a few blissful minutes, my troubles vanished into the myriad bubbles. I loved getting pedicures. Next to sex, there was very little that felt as good, and despite my profession or maybe because of it, sometimes sex slid into second place.

I spent so much time cramming my feet into impossible high heels, a habit I had no intention of changing regardless of what happened with my business. It was heaven to have someone—even someone I paid or maybe especially because it was someone I paid—rub the knots out of my arches. It would be easy to get caught up in the class disparity, but as someone who made her living the way I did, I knew the woman with my foot in her hands didn't need my condescension or pity. She needed my money and honest gratitude. She gave my arch another long stroke, involuntarily curling my toes, and I bit back a groan of disappointment when she set my foot back into the water and reached for her nail shaping tools.

Closing my eyes, I let my mind drift. The problem was, when it drifted, it always seemed to end up back at the eighth and the upcoming interrogatories. Nothing good could come of that. I dug in my pocket and fished out what was left of the roll of antacids, thumbing one off the top. As soon as the fruit-flavored chalk hit my tongue,

I let out my breath and felt my chest relax a fraction of an inch.

My response to the pastel discs had become almost Pavlovian. It was worse than the brief time I'd smoked during college. It had gotten to the point where I couldn't get through my day without the small rolls. The eighth had to hurry up and get here before my habit became an obsession. I sucked on the antacid instead of chewing it and closed my eyes, giving myself over to the slightly ticklish feeling of pale-pink nail polish being painted on my toes. Scarlet or hooker-red would have seemed a more obvious choice, but I'd found that for most of the men I worked with, they liked at least the initial illusion of innocence.

Not that any of that mattered if I lost the business I'd worked so hard to build. I bit down on the antacid, grinding it to powder with my teeth and wishing it was as easy to crush the specter of Erik Jensen and the looming deposition.

ERIK

I'D SPENT MOST of the morning going over the questions for the interrogatory and cementing how I intended to handle Ms. Smithson. All of which got shot to shit the moment I walked into the conference room at Jones and Andrews and saw her sitting at the conference table looking simultaneously frightened and defiant. In her buttoned-up suit and with her wide, dark eyes, she was more cornered cat than sex kitten and damned if she wasn't tempting as hell.

Every bit of her fire and vulnerability pulled at me. I wanted to cradle her in my arms until she felt safe and bend her over the table, shove up her skirt and fuck her senseless all at the same time. I wanted to save her from the monsters and be the monster in the same breath. I was so fucking screwed. And by proxy, so was my client if I couldn't get my shit together.

"Ms. Ellis. Ms. Smithson," I said, managing a curt nod to her counsel without allowing myself to meet Alexandra's scared eyes. I needed to get a fucking grip on myself before I could do that. Sliding into the cool indifference I'd cultivated over the years was as comfortable as putting on an old coat and gave me a chance to re-establish the necessary professional distance between me and the woman I wanted to simultaneously worship and devour.

"Mr. Jensen," said Ms. Ellis.

Alexandra stayed silent, and I was grateful not to have to deal with the way it felt to hear my name on her lips for a little while longer.

The stenographer adjusted her chair, started the recorder and we were off to the races.

"Ms. Smithson, are you the owner of the entity operating as the Gentleman's Submissive?"

"Yes," she said. She started to add more, but caught herself. Ms. Ellis must have coached her to only answer my questions without elaborating.

"And what is it the Gentleman's Submissive does? What services do you offer?" I sat back a little in my chair, waiting to see how she would dance around the illicit nature of her business. She couldn't incriminate herself by admitting to accepting money for sexual services, and since I hadn't found any irregularities or problems with her business license or permits—she was operating under the same constraints sexual surrogates used—I assumed she must have developed a standard answer.

"I train Dominants," she said, leaning forward. "Much in the way a life coach works, I help men—and occasionally women—find and develop their dominant natures."

"You honestly believe you can train Doms?" I asked. The question was out of my mouth before I had a chance to consider it, and I always considered everything, especially where the law was concerned. This case—this woman—had me twisted up in ways that simply weren't going to work.

"To be honest," she said, and I saw Ms. Ellis lean closer to her, presumably to stop her if she went too far off the rails. "I'm not sure that there is such a thing as a real Dominant or submissive. We all have a bit of both inside us. I simply help the people who come to me develop the side they are most interested in cultivating."

Unfucking believable. Here I was getting worked up because she was messing around with something she clearly didn't understand, and the reality was she didn't even seem sure she believed in what she was selling. I'd bet big money that she not only hadn't experienced real submission with a true dominant, she didn't believe it existed.

"So you don't think you are a submissive?"

She actually had the audacity to snort when she laughed.

"No. I mean, I know there are people who believe they are but it's not me. I saw a need and worked out a way to fill it. That's all. It has little to do with my actual temperament and more to do with putting my degree to use."

"And what degree is that?" I asked, not sure what I expected to hear.

"I have a doctorate in gender studies."

Of course she did, and down the rabbit hole we went.

"Forgive me, Ms. Smithson—or perhaps Dr. Smithson is more accurate." I watched her, waiting to see if my condescension would ruffle her feathers, but if anything, it seemed to have the opposite effect. "But could you please explain to me how a PhD in gender studies led you to believe you can train Dominants?" I honestly wasn't sure *what* the degree qualified her for, aside from becoming a professor who taught gender studies.

She leaned forward in her chair, and I couldn't help but notice the way the ivory silk moved and draped over her skin. Her blouse was modest—conservative even—but something about knowing there was nothing but a soft, whisper-thin bit of fabric hiding her lush curves had my mouth going uncharacteristically dry. Her skirt was camel colored today and pencil straight, more suited to a librarian than a woman who made her living cultivating the sexual desires of others. I was just grateful the conference table hid her legs. The last thing my lust-addled brain needed was a clear view of her delicate ankles and what I was sure was another killer pair of fuck-me heels.

"As I already stated for the record, Mr. Jensen, I don't believe I can train Dominants. What my doctorate did was give me valuable insight into the hearts and desires of many women and as a result, to the men who care about them."

I didn't know whether she simply decided to be done being scared of me, or if she hit her stride talking about something she felt passionately about. Either way, the last remnants of her fear seemed to have burned away in the intensity of her gaze. If I wanted her when she was timid, she was magnificent nearing her full power.

"The desire to dominate and submit has become so ingrained in popular culture. It's pervasive in books and movies. Contemporary fiction is full of examples. It was an easy step to see what people wanted, and realize there would be many of them who wouldn't know how to get there. I help men take that final step. To learn to give their partners some of what they need. I provide a service, Mr. Jensen. One that is in increasing demand."

She said my name, and I swallowed hard. I was supposed to be the one turning the tables on her, not the other way around. I glanced down at my notes, scrambling for a question that would give me a moment to find my footing again. In my personal and professional life, I was the one in control and I liked it that way. Hell no, I needed it that way. Nothing about this day was turning out the way I expected.

"Do you have any employees?"

"No, it's just me."

"But what about security?" I asked, going off script yet again. "Surely in your line of work, you must have some mechanism in place to protect you from potentially dangerous clients." If she said no, I was going to have to sit on my hands to keep from shaking her. The idea of her inadvertently putting herself at the mercy of one of the many crazies out there made my jaw clench, and I could feel my blood pressure spike.

"I have a screening process in place before I take on a new client. If I have any reservations at all, I will subcontract security for our first session."

"Perfect. So they have to wait until the second session to let the crazy show," I muttered to myself.

"What?"

"Nothing," I said, forcing myself to move on to what the Dom in me and not the lawyer really wanted to know. "What does a typical session consist of?"

"I'm not sure how that's relevant, Counselor," said Ms. Ellis.

It probably wasn't, but this was part of discovery and not a trial. As such, I had more leeway in my line of questioning.

"In order to understand the extent to which your client is infringing on my client's brand, I need to establish exactly what constitutes a session with the Gentleman's Submissive." I was laying on the bullshit pretty thick. I knew it and I could tell by the pit bull set of Ms. Ellis's pink lacquered lips that she knew it too. The challenge, however, seemed to have taken some of the steam out of Dr. Smithson. She straightened in her chair, looking slightly wary. *Good.* I wanted to know exactly what she was playing at and keeping her off-balance seemed like the best way to find out. "So tell me, Dr. Smithson, what exactly do you do during one of your sessions?"

She glanced to her attorney and then back to me, her brown eyes wide behind the inky fringe of her lashes. Her lips parted but no sound came out and when I saw her hands go white-knuckled on the arms of her chair, it was over for me. I was done.

"Perhaps you'd rather simply show me? Take me through a typical new client session. If there's nothing illicit going on and you have nothing to hide, why not just show me?"

"That's enough, Counselor." I knew Ms. Ellis was objecting, but her voice barely registered.

My entire focus—every atom in my body—shifted to Alexandra and the way she sat frozen in place like a rabbit in front of a wolf. I could be a wolf. Lord knows I'd been called much worse.

"If you are so sure you know enough about the BDSM lifestyle to take men's money to train them to be Doms, then surely you have no reason not to show me— and the court," I added, although in that moment I couldn't have cared less about the case or my trumped-up client. All I cared about was getting Alexandra alone and putting her through her paces. Showing her just the edge of everything she didn't know. "I'm sure I could get Judge Black to order you to follow through as a condition of the suit." It was utter bullshit. Judge Black was no more likely to order Alexandra to take me through a session than he was to suggest we move the trial up a month and hold it in Tahiti. But my words worked. Behind the fear in Alexandra's gaze was a thin sliver of challenge. I'd double-dog dared her and she didn't strike me as the kind of woman who'd let a challenge go unanswered.

"That's enough, Mr. Jensen," said Ms. Ellis, leaning far enough forward in her chair to put her in my line of sight and interrupt my view of Alexandra worrying her bottom lip, her small white teeth dragging against the plump, pink flesh.

"I withdraw."

"The question? Good," said Ms. Ellis, so angry she was practically vibrating.

I didn't blame her. My whole line of questioning had veered completely out of line. I didn't care. I wanted to know—no, needed to know—what was going on in Alexandra's pretty head.

"No, I withdraw from the case," I said, not believing the words until I heard them from my own mouth. It would be tricky, but since I'd been the one pushing for the litigation, I shouldn't have any trouble getting Judge Black to let me off the case. There'd be hell to pay with the other partners, but it was a chance I was more than willing to take.

4

Alex

I RODE THE ELEVATOR TO the street level of Charlotte's building, still shaking from the confrontation with Jensen. His hatred for me and my business felt much too personal. A feeling he'd only reinforced by withdrawing from the case. *What was his deal, anyway?*

I'd racked my brain, trying to remember if I'd ever had anything to do with him before the case, but I kept coming up blank. I wouldn't forget a man like Erik Jensen. I doubted anyone would—woman or man. The man made an impression. Which still didn't answer my questions about why he seemed to be gunning for me and what the hell he'd been thinking, making it personal.

Despite the slightly unorthodox nature of my career choice, I was proud of what I did, and I had a list of satisfied clients to prove it. Of course, until I got out from under this damn lawsuit, the list would shrivel to nothing. Before I left her office, I'd grilled Charlotte about what Jensen pulling himself off my case meant. She seemed as stunned as I was, which was saying something. Charlotte was a Titan. In her element, I'd never seen her show an emotion I wasn't sure she'd intended to show. She'd tried to shake it off and had managed to convince me that

Jensen withdrawing could only help my case, but I couldn't tell if she meant it or if she was trying to save my nerves.

I was grateful for either, I thought, digging into my bag for another roll of the chalky fruit-flavored antacid that was my constant companion. I managed to peel the paper back on a new roll as the elevator doors slid open. Thumbing one of the discs into my mouth, I stepped out into the lobby and almost ran into Erik Jensen.

"What do you want?" I asked, moving back so quickly I almost stumbled. The last thing I wanted was to give the man another excuse to touch me.

He moved with me, closing the distance between us, the look in his eyes positively predatory.

"What the fuck's your problem? You withdrew. As far as I'm concerned, that means we're finished."

Charlotte had at least been clear about that when she explained to me what it meant that Jensen had withdrawn. She'd even used words like *disbar*. He couldn't possibly hate me enough to risk that. He didn't know me.

"No, Dr. Smithson, we're nowhere near finished."

He reached for my elbow, attempting to steer me through the lobby. The practiced ease with which he moved made it clear he was used to doing just that. Steering. Leading. Controlling. I doubt he'd had a woman complain before. His touch was firm and commanding, and if I wasn't so damned confused and pissed off, I might have liked the way his strong fingers dug gently into the tender skin above my elbow. I didn't like it—or at least I didn't want to and that was enough. I made a show of yanking my arm out of his grip and moving away from him.

When I squared my shoulders and looked up to meet his gaze, instead of the anger or, at a minimum, irritation I expected to see, I found amusement. The smug bastard actually looked like he was laughing at me. *Fuck that*. I was through being treated like a child. He'd patronized the hell out of me during the interrogatories, at least before he'd gone off his rails.

"I don't know what the hell crawled up your ass or why you've decided to direct your personal vendetta toward me, but you and I are done." I lifted my chin, daring him to contradict me, and then turned back to the door outside. I'd walk away from him, catch a cab home and lose myself for the time being in the luxury of a long, hot bath. And I'd never have to talk to Erik Jensen again.

"Do you remember Kyle Sondheim, Dr. Smithson? Or has your *client* list grown so extensive that they all run together?"

His mocking tone when he said *client* made me want to punch the smug smirk off his face, but my curiosity was stronger. Kyle had been a client. When he'd come to me, he'd practically been afraid of his own shadow. We'd done a session a week for three months and by the end of our time together, he seemed like a different man. I'd been proud of the work I'd done with Kyle.

"Why do you want to know?" I asked, determined not to surrender anything to this man.

"He was a client of yours?"

He asked the question like he already knew the answer, which I didn't doubt he did. My question was how. Client confidentiality was the foundation of what I did. I wouldn't have a business without it. The only way he could have found out about my work with Kyle was from the man himself. And if he was half as pleased with our results as he had been at our last session, I couldn't imagine what he could have said to Jensen to cause such animosity.

"I can't tell you that, and you know it."

"Ah," he said, rocking back on his heels. "Now you've developed some standards. Pity it's too late."

"You don't know anything about me or my standards. What makes you think you're qualified to judge me?" I spat out the words, layering them with as much disdain as I felt. I was done being lectured by this overbearing pompous asshole of a man.

He took a step closer, then another, and I forced myself to hold my ground. I wouldn't give him the satisfaction of making me back down.

"I am a Dom, Dr. Smithson," he said, standing so close to me I could feel the heat radiating off his tall, hard body.

I couldn't take a breath without being inundated by the rich, spicy scent of expensive cologne and powerful man, but I'd be damned if I let him intimidate me. Then his words cut through the fog his nearness was making of my brain and I snorted. A decidedly unladylike sound. My mother would be so disappointed.

"You don't really believe that, do you?"

The flare of his nostrils was the only indication I had as to how he felt about what I'd said, but he didn't give an inch. He simply stood, completely invading my personal space. I caved, not willing to face the intensity I saw in his gaze and hating myself a little bit for it.

"You don't have to believe in gravity, Dr. Smithson. It simply is, regardless of your perception of it. Mr. Sondheim was a guest at a club I frequent."

I could tell by the care he used to pick his words that there was more than he was telling me, but I wasn't about to let myself be sidetracked.

"And your point is?" Apparently we both had secrets we needed to keep.

"It's a BDSM club, Dr. Smithson. Mr. Sondheim was engaged in a scene with his partner and took things too far. He was calling your name as the bouncers had to physically remove him from the club, insisting that Lexi taught him what to do."

My momentary fascination with the fact that Jensen considered himself a real Dom and frequented BDSM clubs evaporated as the rest of his words sunk in. *Kyle had done something so over the line, he'd gotten himself kicked out of a club.* Mouth dry and heart hammering in my throat, I asked the question I needed to know but was afraid to hear the answer.

"Was his partner hurt?" My voice sounded rough but given the sick uneasiness settling in my stomach, it was lucky I could speak at all.

"Not permanently," he said.

The band around my chest relaxed a fraction of an inch.

"This time," he added. "So I'm going to ask you again, Dr. Smithson, what the fuck makes you think you are qualified to teach anyone about dominance and submission, or anything else for that matter? Have you ever actually worked with a real Dom? Oh, that's right."

He sneered at me and I felt much smaller than my five-foot-four inches. "You don't believe there is such a thing."

"I worked with a Dom." I felt like a petulant child defending myself, and I hated it.

It was his turn to snort. "For how long? How long, Ms. Smithson?" he repeated when I didn't answer.

"An afternoon," I said and braced myself for the explosion I knew would follow.

"Fuck." Jensen ran a hand through his dark hair. "You foolish little girl. You spent an afternoon with someone who claimed to be a Dom and believed you knew enough to teach something you don't even believe in. Unfucking believable."

I should have done more. I'd played voyeur at some clubs up north and gone to a couple of munches. I'd read everything I could get my hands on, from *The Loving Dominant* to a library's worth of popular genre fiction, but I'd never become part of a community. I knew when I'd started an afternoon of hands-on practice wasn't enough, but it had been hard to find someone who called himself a Dom and who actually seemed to have some idea what he was doing. In the end, I couldn't bring myself to give control over to someone else and the whole experience left me feeling very uncomfortable. After I'd started the business and hit my stride, I figured I knew enough to get the job done. My clients certainly seemed to think so.

"Take me through one of your sessions." He somehow managed to make the rest of the lobby disappear until we were the only ones left and the only things I could concentrate on were the sound of his voice and his dark eyes pinning me in place.

"I can't do that," I said, giving my head a shake to try to clear it. The man was too damn much. Too big, too strong, just too there. "My clients demand confidentiality."

"I don't want to watch, Dr. Smithson." The corner of his lip curved up in that sexy pirate sneer and my traitorous body decided to take notice. "Pretend I'm a client. Hell, I'll pay you if it makes you feel better."

I thought about Jensen on the other end of the flogger and something that felt a hell of a lot like desire wound low and warm inside me. I checked my reaction, clenching my jaw and forcing my expression into what I hoped looked neutral and not crazed. Taking the dangerous man through a session was a colossally bad idea. I opened my mouth to tell him but he interrupted before I got the *no* out.

"What are you scared of? If you're so sure you know what you're doing, taking me through a session should be a cakewalk."

Everything from the set of his shoulders to his arched eyebrow—hell, even the way he said doctor as if it were an insult, not an honor—screamed challenge. I made it a point of pride never to back down from a challenge, but the idea of taking Jensen through one of my typical sessions made my stomach knot. Or it could completely turn the tables. He'd obviously lost his mind earlier, which meant despite his cool exterior, he wasn't immune. And even though I'd be the one mostly naked, I'd found, with most men at least, that gave me more of the power. I'd ignore for now the fact that Jensen didn't strike me as anything like most men.

"Come on, Dr. Smithson. I dare you."

"You dare me? What are we, back in middle school?"

"The way you're handling it, we may as well be. So tell me, are you woman enough to show me what you do?" He stepped back, giving the illusion at least that he would abide by my choice. "Or are you going to run away and continue to play dress up like a little girl until someone really gets hurt?"

Well, hell. I'd like to think I was enough of an adult not to let myself be goaded into something as stupid as taking the arrogant attorney through a session just to save my pride, but I couldn't ignore the feeling that I was responsible for what had happened to Kyle. When he'd come to see me, he seemed like such a sweet, careful man. I didn't understand how he could have gotten things so wrong, and I hated that he thought it was because of something he'd learned from me. I wouldn't forgive myself if it happened again and someone else got hurt. I couldn't let that happen. Which meant taking on Jensen. *Fuck.*

"Fine," I said, regretting the word as soon as it left my mouth. "We can set up an appointment for *one* session."

His expression turned triumphant and for a second, I felt like a gazelle negotiating with a tiger.

"Our appointment is in twenty minutes," he said, taking my arm again and moving me through the doors and out onto the street. "I'm not giving you a chance to come up with some kind of bullshit excuse."

The driver got out of a black town car parked in front of the building and opened the door for me.

"Where to, Mr. Jensen?" he asked, tipping his hat to the marauder in a designer suit behind me.

"Wherever the lady says."

Both men waited and my stumbling brain finally caught up. This is where I told him I was sorry. I'd lost my mind for a moment but we wouldn't be having a session. Instead, I heard the address to my studio come out of my mouth a second before Jensen handed me into the back of the car, sliding in after.

ERIK

I STILL COULDN'T quite believe Alexandra had agreed to my proposition, but the car headed across town toward the address she'd given. Either it was her studio or she'd worked up some kind of switch—unlikely given how quickly she'd told the driver where to go, but not impossible.

I should be furious and I was, but my emotions were frustratingly more complicated than that. The imposter Dom trainer with a PhD in gender studies had me so twisted up; I'd let my feelings get in the way of my work. I could try to convince myself it was all because of what happened at Bacchus and the danger I thought Dr. Smithson presented, but the way my body thrummed to life sitting in the backseat next to her told a different story. I wanted her submission—given willingly—in a way I hadn't since before Julie left.

Hell, maybe it was longer than that. Watching the way her breath hitched every time my thigh brushed hers and the pretty pink flush to her cheeks, I couldn't remember wanting anyone more. The fact that I was almost positive she was a closet submissive who didn't know it and I was going to be the one to show her only made the prospect that much more delicious. I couldn't wait to make her beg and then be the one to give her everything she needed. I had to keep reminding myself that she wasn't an ordinary hookup, and I had a more important agenda than making her come so many times she forgot her own name.

The car pulled up in front of the address she'd given the driver and Alexandra scooted to the edge of her seat, ready to spring from the car. The building looked clean, well-maintained, and surprisingly modern for its location just outside the Quarter. I exited the car first, catching and holding her hand as she climbed out after me. I could feel the energy practically vibrating off her. She was like a bird ready to take off, and I had a sudden image of her bound, naked and tied open for me while I figured out how to help her fly.

I had to get my shit together. Letting my imagination run wild wouldn't get me what I wanted—Dr. Smithson to realize she was playing with powers she didn't understand and to make a career change before someone got hurt. Shaking my head, I watched her punch in a code, automatically cataloguing the numbers in my head. It was one of the coping mechanisms I'd come up with working my way through law school. Numbers were still a thousand times easier than letters, which only mattered if the lawyer thing didn't work out and I had to turn to a life of crime. Reading might be a challenge for me, but I had the kind of memory that made counting cards and memorizing numbers as easy as breathing. She opened the door, giving me a nervous glance over her shoulder before entering.

With its dark wood trim and architectural details, the interior of the building felt more in keeping with the city but none of that in and of itself was remarkable. The only thing that caught my attention was the surprising lack of security. Aside from having to know the code to enter the building, there wasn't anything to stop any psycho she might pick up from making his way at least as far as the elevator. Thinking of her bringing someone she didn't know to this space set my teeth on edge.

"You bring clients here? To this building? By yourself?" I asked, hoping the answer was no.

"We already covered that during the deposition, Counselor. The kind of work I do requires a certain amount of privacy and discretion." As she spoke, her shoulders shifted and the blushing woman from the car was gone, replaced by someone sure of herself and her work. *The woman was a fucking chameleon.*

"I'm amazed you've lasted this long." My thoughts ran to images from reality crime scenes, and I had to clench my fists to keep from shaking some sense into her or pulling her into me to shelter against my body. The urge to protect her was becoming much too frequent and damned inconvenient.

She shot me a look that screamed *Oh please* before getting into the elevator and pushing the button for the second floor. Every step we took away from the world outside made it that much clearer what kind of risks she was taking. *Unacceptable* risks.

"I've lived in this city since I graduated from school. I'm not stupid and I'm not naïve."

I snorted in disbelief and she turned the full force of her dark eyes on me.

"Listen, you patronizing asshole. I screen my clients thoroughly and I hire security for the first session, longer if I get any hint that I need it. *You* don't care more about my safety than I do. I'm taking a bigger chance bringing you here than I've ever taken with a client. They've all been harmless."

I hated her answer. She was playing with fire and didn't realize it, but I loved that she recognized I was dangerous. Not to her physical safety. I'd never take things further than she wanted to go. But I had every intention of pushing her outside her comfort zone and challenging every belief she held about herself. Before we were done with each other, she'd know Doms and submissives were real and she'd know exactly which side of the line we each stood on.

Pushing aside thoughts of her slack-ass security system to revisit later, I placed my hand on the small of her back, partly because I knew my touch unnerved her and maybe even more significant, simply because I wanted to touch her. To feel the curve of her waist and the heat of her body through the thin silk of her blouse. She hurried through the open doors, obvious—if unsuccessful—in her desire to step away from my touch.

A solid wooden door stood opposite the elevator. The intertwined script initials GS were the only indication of what went on inside. Alexandra punched in another code, took a deep breath and pushed the door open. We jostled for a few moments, each of us insisting the other enter first. I finally walked into the room, content to give her the illusion of control, at least for a few minutes.

The room was stark but beautiful, with ebony wood floors and cool white walls. The lack of decoration added importance to the few pieces in the room. Alexandra had the image down pat. It would have made a better set for my client's movie than the cheesy dungeon they'd used to shoot. *Ex-client*, I reminded myself. A wooden St. Andrew's Cross took up the prominent spot in the room, flanked on one side by a huge, elaborately carved armoire and a padded leather horse on the other. The cuffs on the cross were Velcro, but the metal rings at the base of the horse were welded in place. The idea of her binding her wrists and ankles, making herself helpless in front of some stranger, made me want to thrash her myself. My thoughts must have shown on my face— another clear sign of how twisted up she had me—because she opened a drawer on the armoire and pulled out a pair of cuffs.

"I always use my own cuffs. Quick release," she said, holding them out so I could see the button that opened them without a key.

It was smart, if inadequate, but it also meant she'd never really felt helpless. At least not in this room. The irony of wanting her safe and in control and helpless at the same time hit me like a punch to the gut, but I'd have to sort out my feelings later. Dr. Smithson and I had work to do first.

She set the cuffs back in the drawer and when she turned around to face me, she'd changed again, sliding into what I assumed was her Lexi persona. It was the same way she'd looked when we met outside the judge's chambers— the guise of a sex kitten with the demeanor of a Dominatrix. She might be playing a game she didn't believe in, but she had some skill. Too bad it was all in the wrong direction and dangerous enough that someone could get hurt.

"This is where I hold my sessions," she said, motioning to the room around her. "Under regular circumstances, we'd have a consultation, and I'd know what you wanted to work on before we started, but since you're an unusual case, we'll have to play this a bit by ear."

She stalked toward me, putting a little extra swing into her hips and closing the distance between us. Keeping her gaze locked on mine, she let her hand rest on my arm and leaned in close enough for me to smell the heady floral scent she wore.

"Normally, I'd have had you submit a doctor's report and sign a non-disclosure agreement before you saw the inside of this room, but I think we know things about each other that we'd both rather not be made public, so I'm comfortable proceeding." She laced the word *comfortable* with enough sexual energy to make it feel like it meant something much more than *okay*. "I charge two hundred dollars for the consultation and two thousand dollars for the first session. Since this is an unorthodox situation, I'll waive the consultation fee. You can PayPal Lexi at the Gentleman's Submissive dot com. It's spelled the way you say it."

She pursed her gorgeous fuckable lips and blinked up at me. *That's why she was so calm. She didn't expect me to go through with it.* She must have assumed when it came time to pay up, I'd walk and let her off the hook. Grinning, I pulled my phone from my pocket and made quick work of sending the payment. In a few seconds, her phone chimed, I assume announcing the money's arrival. She grabbed the phone from her bag and glanced at the screen, a wrinkle forming in the center of her forehead.

"Are we set?" I asked, feeling like the fucking Big Bad Wolf watching Red make her way through the forest.

I saw her swallow and then nod. "What would you like to work on? Since you say you're already a Dom, you have to give me some idea where you'd like to start." She said the word *Dom* with the same intonation I imagined she'd use to describe someone from Mars.

My anger at her and her business practices had morphed into something darker. More intriguing. I was going to enjoy every minute of this.

"How much time do we have?" I asked, running through possibilities in my head. Hell, I'd drop another two grand if I had to to teach Dr. Smithson what she didn't understand.

"Sessions usually run for two to three hours, depending on what a client wants to work on."

"I see the obvious choices." I motioned to the cross and the bench. "Why don't you show me what you have in your toy box?"

She nodded, the press of her lips into a thin line the only sign she was uncomfortable. Opening the wooden doors, she revealed an impressive array of floggers, paddles, and crops. Most of it was what you'd expect to find at a typical adult toy store—nothing as hard as a cane or whip, thank fuck. There were shelves holding a variety of vibrators, dildos, and plugs and two smaller drawers. I scanned the cabinet, keeping part of my attention on her so I could gage her reaction as I looked at each item. She didn't blink when I studied the floggers but I saw her suck in a breath when I moved closer to the items on the shelves. When I nodded toward the drawers, her pulse kicked up enough I could see it beat against the delicate skin of her throat.

"Open them please," I asked, deliberately keeping my hands behind my back. When I finally reached for something, I wanted the added visual impact.

She slid open the top drawer, revealing her trick cuffs and a few blindfolds I was fairly certain she'd be able to see through. She paused for a moment with her hand resting on the drawer below. Inhaling, she opened the drawer and took a step away from it and me. *Interesting.* A modest selection of clamps and intimate jewelry lay nestled on a red velvet pad. With the delicate chains and beads, it looked much tamer than the clover clamps and weighted clips routinely used at the club, but either she'd had a bad experience with it or she wanted to try it. With the way she ran away from who she was, I could only guess. It didn't matter. We were a long way from nipple clamps.

"May I?" I asked, not bothering to hide my grin when her cheeks flushed.

She nodded without speaking and I reached into the cabinet and pulled out a soft leather flogger. When I turned back to face her, I caught her staring at my hand wrapped around the braided leather handle. I took a step toward her, watching her struggle to keep from backing up.

"Is this what you normally wear for a session?"

"No." She broke down and took a step back, but when she met my eyes again, she'd clearly found her footing. While I watched, she made quick work of the buttons on her blouse, letting the silk fall open to reveal an almost demure white bra and inch after inch of creamy skin.

I could tell she was used to taking her clothes off and used to the effect her body had on men. It was a sacrifice, but I kept my gaze on her face, ignoring the delicious lace-covered breasts I wanted covered with just my hands or my mouth. She shrugged out of the blouse and walked to the horse, draping the ivory silk over the leather before turning back to face me. Pulling her bottom lip between her teeth, she reached behind her, arching her back to emphasize her fucking perfect tits. A moment later, the pencil skirt dropped to the floor, leaving her in nothing but a few scraps of lace and the fuck-me heels that I wanted to feel digging into my ass as I took her up against the wall. She dropped into a crouch that would have done a pole dancer proud, snagged her skirt and turned her back to me, ostensibly so she could drape her skirt over the horse, but more, I was sure, so I got a good look at her thong.

"Normally, I let the client choose the color," she said, adjusting the thin strip of lace riding low on her hips as she glanced over her shoulder at me. "But these are unusual circumstances."

She reached up to pull the pins from her hair and let it cascade down her back in a wave. She shook it out before sectioning it and made quick work of braiding it into a long, thick plait. Taking a band she'd snagged from somewhere, she bound the end of her ponytail. I tightened my grip on the flogger so I wouldn't reach out to wrap her dark hair around my fist.

Alexandra Smithson clearly knew how to wield sex for power, and she was damned good at it. I didn't have any doubt that she intended to use every move she made to put me deeper under her spell. She might be mostly naked, but she wasn't vulnerable. She worked her body like a weapon, one I imagined slayed most men. Good thing I wasn't most men.

Before she turned around to face me, she unclasped her bra and tossed it carelessly over the horse with the rest of her clothes. Calling on every trick I'd learned over the years in the courtroom and out, I schooled my face and watched her pivot on the toes of her fuck-me heels. The look on her face said she clearly expected to have the upper hand, and there was no way in hell that was going to happen.

Running the soft leather tails of the flogger through my fingers, I dropped my gaze to her feet and worked my way up every inch of her glorious body. I took long enough to drink in my fill and make her just uncomfortable enough to subtly shift her weight from one foot to the other. I wouldn't have picked up on it if I hadn't been watching her so closely. By the time my eyes met hers, I knew exactly what I wanted to do with her. By the time we finished, she'd be begging for me to touch her.

In two strides, I closed the distance between us. Her breath hitched, making her fucking fantastic tits move and for a second, her gaze darted to the flogger in my hand. Then she licked her lips, feigning a bravado I was sure she didn't feel.

"What are your limits, Alexandra?"

Her gaze met mine and I saw a flash of uncertainty shining in her eyes.

"I'm not sure what you mean."

I shook my head, not bothering to hide my judgment. She was a child playing a very dangerous game. If she insisted on acting like a child, I had no problem treating her like one.

"Are your clients allowed to mark you or touch you with anything other than the toys? What kind of intimate contact do you allow and where?" Considering the array of goodies in her wardrobe and her reaction to them, I had a pretty good idea what she was willing to do, but I loved watching her blush when I asked the question.

"It depends," she said, her voice cracking. "If it's necessary for a session, then yes." She swallowed hard, but her gaze met mine and I could tell she wouldn't back down.

I gave her my best cocky grin, getting off on the shift in power.

"It's necessary, kitten."

Alex

FUCK. I'D STOOD IN FRONT of Erik Jensen wearing nothing but a G-string and heels and he hadn't so much as blinked. With the exception of that long look that ran over my body like a caress, he'd barely glanced at me.

It's not that I'm vain. I have an extra ten pounds to lose and areas on my body that I hate, just like every other woman. But one of the things I've learned running the Gentleman's Submissive and getting naked in front of men was that they don't care. Like at all. Put a pair of halfway decent naked breasts in front of them and most of them have trouble remembering their own names. They're lost, making the visual equivalent of *gimme* hands. A few extra pounds or cottage cheese thighs don't hit the radar. They truly don't care.

I've gotten very comfortable with my body, not because I thought I looked so great. Simply because I realized the naked one has the power. I might be flashing my tits but the guy in the suit is the one suffering from lack of blood to the brain. At least that had been the case for every man except Erik fucking Jensen.

He wasn't even supposed to be here. I never intended for things to go so far. I figured I'd give him the price, demand twice my normal payment and watch him scurry away. It honestly hadn't occurred to me that he'd actually cough up the money, but even after that, I should've been able to handle things. Strip off my clothes, watch the counselor's brain go soft while the rest of him got hard and wait out our time.

Except it wasn't his brain that turned to mush; it was mine every time I caught a glimpse of his wrist resting against the handle of the damn flogger, looking as comfortable with it in his hand as if he'd used it every day. And now he was talking about touching me and limits and calling me kitten, and I didn't know what to hope for. The only thing I knew for sure was that he was different than any other client I'd ever worked with.

"Stand still," he said, pinning me with his much too-perceptive gaze.

I'd used every trick I could think of to project a confidence I didn't feel, but I didn't think it mattered. I had a feeling Jensen could see through every mask I put on. I froze, working hard to keep from fidgeting on my heels. Wearing less than a pocket square's worth of fabric, I stood in front of him and waited. He crossed his arms over his chest, the tails of the flogger juxtaposed against the custom cut of his suit, emphasizing the businessman-turned-pirate vibe I'd gotten earlier. He was gorgeous, sexy and strong, and barely civilized and for reasons I was not willing to look at too closely, I wanted to please him. I waited for him to tell me what came next because I wanted to know.

I'd spent plenty of time in my studio wearing nothing more than a G-string, but for the first time, standing in front of him with Erik watching me, I felt naked. It was nerve-racking, and overwhelming, and delicious all at the same time, and the longer we stood there facing each other, the stronger the feeling got.

"You are so beautiful," he said and the honest appreciation in his voice washed over me like a caress. "Do you trust me?"

My smirk answered the question for me, and he laughed, a deep throaty chuckle that tightened something low in my body.

"Let me rephrase that. Do you trust me not to hurt you? Do you feel physically safe with me?"

I didn't have to think about that one. I wouldn't have brought him to the studio if I hadn't known I was safe with him. Well, not *safe* exactly. I had a feeling I was in way over my head and if this went where I thought it was going, I was pretty sure much of what I believed would be shredded and replaced with something else. But I also knew he wouldn't hurt me and I believed he'd respect my limits. I wanted to find out. It felt as if I was standing on the edge of something, peering over, and I wanted to see the other side. At a bare minimum, I owed it to my clients. At least that was the bullshit lie I told myself. In reality, it was Alex, not Lexi, who wanted to find out what it would be like with a man like Erik.

"Yes." I nodded, agreeing to more than the question he'd asked.

"Good." He set the flogger aside and reached for the knot of his tie.

My mouth practically watered in anticipation as he loosened the silk. He pulled the tie free of his collar with a snap, and I sucked in a breath, anxious to get a glimpse of the hard body hidden under his custom suit. I had an idea of how strong he was from the way he'd caught me when

I'd stumbled. I couldn't wait to see if the reality matched my imagination.

He popped open the button at his collar, revealing a triangle of tanned skin. Instead of shedding his jacket like I'd expected, he closed the distance between us, still holding the tie in his hands.

I felt naked and vulnerable. I wanted him to go away, and I wanted him to touch me. It was a race to see which feeling was stronger.

"You're going to need a safe word," he said, and all the breath left my body.

Honestly, what the fuck was I expecting? Of course, I needed a safe word. It's just that I was usually the one telling clients that, explaining things and soothing their nerves. Jensen didn't need me to explain anything, but I had a feeling he was going to expect something I'd never given. My surrender. I'd spent a significant amount of time playing submissive to help my clients get in touch with their dominant sides, but I'd never actually submitted. I might be the naked one, but I controlled what happened in the studio.

I topped from the bottom, and I didn't know if I was ready to change that. The alternative was walking away, and no matter how I'd felt in the beginning, I was too curious to turn away now.

"Mercy," I said, hoping I hadn't just bit off more that I could chew. "My safe word is mercy."

"Good girl." He reached up to cup my cheek and I bloomed at his praise, ignoring the fact that I was naked as I leaned into his touch.

What the hell? I didn't have daddy issues. I grew up in an upper middle-class home with two parents and basically no conflict. Nobody'd molested me. Growing up, my parents had been proud of me and told me so. I wasn't starving for some man's approval. I never had been. So what was up with the way my body reacted to Jensen? He commanded, and I wanted to comply. I didn't understand it and I didn't like it. Or rather, my mind didn't like it. My body was on board with any plan the arrogant attorney had, as evidenced by the fact that I was practically squirming to keep from throwing myself into his arms.

"Close your eyes, Alexandra."

God, I loved the way it sounded when he said my name. I did what he said and felt him move to stand behind me. Curiosity and nerves made me tremble, and when I finally felt the silk touch my face, I jumped.

"Easy. I'll take care of you," he said, his breath hot against my ear.

Again with the words I shouldn't want to hear. I was more than capable of taking care of myself. But I'd have to clue my body in quick. Despite what I thought, my body seemed eager to let Jensen take the lead.

"If you want to stop or if any of this gets to be too much, I want you to use your safe word. I mean it, Alexandra. This is your first time."

I let out an unladylike noise at the idea that I was some kind of innocent. I made my living taking off my clothes. If you took skydiving, climbing the Himalayas, and threesomes out of the mix, I didn't have all that many firsts left.

Erik wrapped his fist around my ponytail and gave it a gentle tug. Not hard enough to hurt, just enough to bring my attention firmly back to the present.

"Trust me," he said, pressing his body along my back, his lips barely a breath from my ear. "I can tell. What do you say if you want me to stop?"

"Mercy," I said over the whooshing sound of my heartbeat in my ears.

Damn, I was actually going to do this thing. He wrapped what I assumed was his tie over my eyes and cinched it tight against my head. When he stepped away from me, the urge to try to peek past the silk was almost overwhelming. I started trembling as soon as I heard him at the cabinet. With the way he handled the flogger, I assumed that's what he'd want to use. Fuck me for assuming. I knew better.

I hadn't actually used most of the other stuff in the cabinet. It was mainly for show and so clients could see the kind of things their partners were reading about. Like poor Peter, none of them worked up the nerve to try any of the dildos or plugs on me. They weren't even interested in negotiating the terms. It wasn't like I'd been eager to jump into that end of the pool. And if they expressed any curiosity in the clamps or plugs, all I had to do was suggest they try them on themselves first so they understood what it felt like before trying it with a partner. The few souls brave enough to broach the subject turned green at my suggestion and moved on to the less invasive toys. Men were such babies.

Except I hadn't talked about any of that with Jensen and who knew what the hell he was planning. Thinking better of this whole arrangement, I opened my mouth to call things off when I heard the cabinet latch and his steps getting closer.

"Relax, Alexandra." I heard the smile in his voice and I hated the idea that he was laughing at my helplessness. "I can hear you thinking across the room. I won't touch you without telling you what I'm doing first. This time," he said, and I wondered how sure he had to be of himself to assume we'd do anything like this ever again. I heard a swish of fabric and then sensed him standing behind me again, close but not touching. "In order for this to work, I'm going to have to trust you, too. I have to trust you not to cheat and try to look. If we're going to do this, then be honest about it and give yourself over to the experience or use your safe word. Can you do that?"

Well, hell, so much for peeking. I was running out of chances to say no. I thought for a long moment, making sure I could do what he was asking of me, and then I nodded.

"Yes."

"Good," he said, his voice warm with an approval I apparently craved. *Damn it.* "Arms out. I'm going to help you put this on."

I wanted to grill him about what he was doing, but before I got out the first question, I felt the brush of silk over my hand and what I was pretty sure was the sleeve of my blouse being pulled up my arm. Erik repeated the process with my other arm while I stood, stunned, in place and let him dress me like a child.

I'd expected him to take off his clothes and instead he was putting mine back on. Maybe this whole Dom thing was his crazy way of making fun of me. Maybe he was actually gay. I didn't think he was but since when did a dude put clothes on a woman without touching her?

"Are you married?"

"Fuck, no," he said with a laugh. "Close those gorgeous lips of yours before I find something to slip between them."

He'd told me to shut up and figured out how to make it sound sexy. I'd clearly gone off the deep end.

He moved to the front of my body, and I felt the brush of his fingertips. I still wasn't wearing a bra and the silk grazing my nipples combined with his casual, almost impersonal, touch had me squirming on my heels again. Thank God, he let me keep my panties on or I wouldn't be able to hide the effect he had on me. I doubted I was doing all that good of a job anyway. Hiding from Erik seemed pointless. He seemed to have some kind of magic sexual sixth sense.

I felt him close the button at the top of my blouse, the teasing touch of his fingertips maddening as he worked his way between my breasts and over the soft mound of my stomach. My nipples were so hard against the silk of my blouse, they ached. If he'd been any other man, I'd have taken his hands and put them where I needed them. But he wasn't any man and I wasn't ready for him to know how much I wanted him. Not yet. Not until I knew where this thing between us was going. I still wasn't a hundred percent sure he hadn't set up some way to embarrass or make fun of me.

"Your breasts are magnificent," he said as he closed the last button. "I fucking love the way your nipples stand out against the silk—like they're aching for my mouth. Step."

I felt him drop to his knees in front of me, but it took a moment for my lust-addled brain to get past his words and realize he wanted me to step into my skirt. I started to raise one foot and then tottered on my heel, almost stumbling. Without thinking, I reached out to steady myself and my hand landed partly on his shoulder and partly on the warm skin of his neck. My fingertips brushed the curls that skimmed his collar and I had to fight the urge to tunnel my fingers into his hair.

It was an almost irresistible pull, the same kind of pull I'd felt the first night in front of the bar when I'd met his gaze and then later outside the judge's chambers before he knew who I was. It felt electric, like there was some kind of current moving between us, and I exhaled carefully, hoping the effect he had on me wasn't completely obvious. Lack of confidence wasn't the man's problem. He didn't need me doing anything to bolster it.

"Step again," he said, and the rough edge to his voice made me wonder if maybe he'd felt it too. Whatever the fuck *it* was.

Keeping my hand on his shoulder, I stepped with the other foot, working hard to maintain the lie that I was touching him to keep from falling and not because I liked having my hands on him. He shimmied the skirt over my hips and I sucked in my stomach so he could button it and slide up the zipper. It was crazy, but having him dress me felt more intimate than standing nearly naked in front of him.

Grasping my hips in his hands, he rested his forehead against the soft mound of my stomach. It was a gesture so unexpectedly tender, I forgot myself for a moment. I slid my fingers into his hair, stroking the soft curls and wondering if I was supposed to be the submissive, why he was the one on his knees.

"Come on, Alexandra," he said. I heard him inhale and then get to his feet. "We're going out."

Alex

"WAIT A MINUTE." THE WARM feelings I'd been having for Jensen evaporated at the idea of leaving the safety of my studio. Blindfolded. It was one thing to stand in my familiar space and not be able to see. Casting aside for a moment all the kinds of crazy I'd look walking around the city with Jensen's tie wrapped around my head, how was I supposed to go anywhere when I couldn't see?

Fuck, the man outmaneuvered me. He'd found a way to really get me to submit. If I didn't want to bounce off walls or risk walking into traffic, I was going to have to let him lead me. I had to trust him and depend on him to keep me safe. I thought we'd play tie me up/tie me down, trade a couple of orgasms and part ways. It felt screwed-up even in my head, but what he expected was so much bigger than what I'd been planning to give him.

Unless I cheated and looked. Which I wouldn't, because he was right. If I was going to do this, I was going to be honest about it.

"Are you ready or do you want to use your safe word?" There was nothing playful about his tone. He wasn't trying to tease me or goad me into this. If I left with him, it would be because I decided to do it.

"No. I mean, yes, I'm ready."

"Good." He leaned closer, and I breathed in the spicy scent of his aftershave. He draped something—his suit coat—over my shoulders. The coat smelled like him and the warmth radiating off it from his body wrapped around me like a caress.

"Why?" I asked, curious why now, when I couldn't see, was the moment he chose to take off a piece of his clothing. It wasn't like it was cold outside.

"Because," he said, closing the last few inches between us until I could feel his breath against my ear. "I don't want anyone but me to know how fucking amazing your tits look with nothing but a wisp of silk over them. Your nipples are already hard and I can see them clearly through the thin fabric. I'm going to be the only one to see them today."

He added the *today*. What else could he say? We weren't even close to anything resembling a couple, and he knew what I did for a living. He couldn't seriously be looking for any kind of exclusivity. But there was something so possessive in his tone and the way his hand held my hip. Despite the warnings my mind was giving me, my body tightened in anticipation.

"You could let me put my bra on." I breathed out the words, turning my head so my cheek brushed against his. That simple touch was enough to make me want more.

"No way. Every time you take a step, I want you to feel the silk drag over your nipples. And Alexandra, I want you to imagine it's my hands on you. My mouth." He slid his hand from my waist up over my rib cage to cup my breast. His hand was hot against my skin and the slide of silk between his flesh and mine enhanced every touch.

I held my breath, wanting so desperately for him to touch my hard nipples. Worried I'd do something stupid—like throw myself at him—I froze in place and waited. With what felt like the pad of his thumb, Erik stroked the pebbled tip, his touch so achingly soft, I could have cried from wanting him. My lips parted on a sigh and then he was kissing me, one hand cupping my breast while the other gripped my ponytail, anchoring me in place while his lips drank from mine.

His touch was firm, demanding, and much too brief. I was still leaning into him, trying to follow him blindly with my lips, when he pulled away. Resting his hands on my shoulders, he gently turned me away from him.

"Okay, there's nothing between you and the door. Let's go."

I expected him to hold my hand at least, but he didn't touch me. He stood behind me and waited for me to move. Either we were going to stand there like that until one of us gave up or I was going to have to start walking.

It's not as easy as you think. Seriously, try it. Close your eyes in a familiar room and start walking. Now do it on four-inch heels with your nipples trying to carve their way out of your blouse. Point made, no pun intended.

I took a tentative step, keeping my hands out in front of me so I wouldn't run into anything. Erik said there wasn't anything in front of me. It was my room. I knew there wasn't anything between me and the wall, but I still shuffle-stepped like Herman Munster across the floor. How was I supposed to keep this up outside? At least we were in the city. People either wouldn't notice or they'd assume it was some kind of performance art. Acceptance of outward craziness was one more thing I loved about my adopted city.

"Keep going," said Erik, startling me and making me almost lose my footing. "Just another couple of steps and you're there."

Easy for him to say. I took a few more tentative steps and sensed the wall before I felt it. I stretched my fingertips out in front of me, inching closer until they grazed the wall. Stepping forward one more time, I rested my palms against the smooth, cool surface of the drywall. Before I had time to worry about what to do next, Erik was behind me, his hands gripping my upper arms and pressing his lips to the tender skin behind my ear. I arched my neck, instinctively moving toward the pleasure, and I felt him chuckle against my skin.

"Beautiful," he said.

I couldn't tell if he meant me or the job I'd done walking blindfolded. I didn't care. I wasn't sure why and I wasn't sure I liked myself for it, but I wanted to please him. It had suddenly become important to me to do this right. Whatever *this* was.

Sliding his hand to the small of my back, he kept up a steady reassuring pressure while I heard the sound of the door opening.

"Careful," he said, gently nudging me forward. "There's a threshold."

I shuffled through the door, stumbling a little when the hard wood of the studio turned into the carpet in the hallway. Erik never left my side, steadying me and steering me toward the elevator. The ding and sound of the doors opening signaled the car's arrival and suddenly everything got very real. It was one thing to stumble around my studio. It was an entirely different thing taking this show on the road. As the elevator came to a stop, my stomach did a little flip, and my nerves ratchetted up to crazy level.

"Tell me where we're going." I hated the slightly desperate edge to my voice, but with the way my heart was pounding in my ears, I'd been lucky to get the words out at all.

"That's not how this works," he said, sounding much too smug.

He'd stopped touching me when we stepped onto the elevator and I'd be damned if I asked him for his help after that comment. The elevator dinged, and gathering a confidence I didn't feel, I took mincing sliding steps in the direction of the door, picking up my feet and stepping over when I felt the threshold with my toes.

I knew this building. I'd walked through it dozens of times before. Ignoring the man hovering just far enough behind me to be of no help, I pictured the lobby in my mind and started across it.

"Easy," warned Erik, closing the distance between us.

Feeling his hand on my back through his jacket, I stopped and reached out in front of me. Closer than I expected, I felt the glass of the door in front of me. I sucked in a breath and pushed the door open.

The first thing I noticed was the noise. In addition to the sounds of traffic passing on the street in front of me, I heard snippets of conversations as people passed by and even the flapping and coos of a few random pigeons. I was always caught up in my own world and never really noticed before, but my city was noisy. And parts of it didn't smell great. The other thing I realized was that I couldn't step onto the sidewalk by myself. Without being able to see, I had no way of knowing who, if anyone, was coming my way. Unless I wanted to risk running into some poor unsuspecting pedestrian, I was going to have to ask Jensen for help.

"Ready?" he asked, his hand still on my back.

"Do I have a choice?" The idea of quitting set my teeth on edge. I hated the idea of asking Jensen for help, but I hated the idea of losing to him even more.

"You always have a choice."

Not if I didn't want to admit he was right, and I was wrong. "Let's go."

With his hand still pressed against the small of my back, he nudged me through the door and out on to the sidewalk. In a testament to the self-absorbed nature of the city I loved and its willingness to embrace the crazy, no one bothered to comment about the strange woman stumbling down the sidewalk wearing a man's jacket and blindfolded with his tie, and if they avoided me or if they looked at me like I'd lost it, I couldn't see, so it didn't matter. In my gorgeous excessive nutbar of a city, it was unlikely anyone would even notice.

"This way, Alexandra." He took me by the shoulders and turned me to the left.

The longer I wore the blindfold, the angrier I got. Wanting to please him had quickly morphed into frustration at having to depend on him for something as basic as not running into walls. I felt shaky and uncertain. Out of control, and I didn't do out of control. Everything in my life, from my grades as a kid to my choice of profession, had been executed according to a carefully controlled plan. If things didn't go the way I wanted them to, I worked harder, removing obstacles until I got where I wanted. So what the hell was I doing, standing somewhere on Rampart at the mercy of a man I barely knew for something as basic as walking down the street?

Except I wasn't at his mercy. Not really. I could take off the blindfold any time and leave Erik standing by himself. I made a choice every second I kept his stupid tie wrapped around my head. I really, really didn't want to know what that said about me. What kind of woman voluntarily surrendered control to a man? And an arrogant fucking know-it-all one at that. Not that my traitorous body seemed to give a fuck what my rational mind thought about him. Just the touch of his hand, strong and sure on the small of my back, sent heat radiating through me, despite the layers of fabric and better judgment between his palm and my flesh. *God bless.* I was in way over my head.

Needing to exert some control and unwilling to do something as simple as taking off the makeshift blindfold, I picked up my pace and stepped just out of his grip. This was my city and my street. I'd walked it hundreds of times before going about my business, getting lunch, meeting Meredith for yoga at Namaste. We'd only gone a block or so—less than two because I'd only had to manage one set of curbs, which meant we were between Iberville and Canal in the block with the praline shop. I took a deep breath, inhaling the delicious aroma of caramelized sugar and toasted pecans. We were a few blocks from the heart of the French Quarter and its crowds of tourists, but at this time of year, there were enough people in my city to spill out of the Quarter and up the side streets. When I focused my attention, I could hear the older woman who ran the shop selling candy to someone with a Midwestern accent.

I didn't care what people thought. If I did, I would never have started my business and I sure as hell wouldn't have made it a success. It took a lot to embarrass me, but I liked Miss Morel's candy. I'd been known to stop in from time to time to get a small paper sack of pralines to nibble on with my afternoon café au lait. The idea of the older woman seeing me being led down the street by the asshole lawyer didn't sit right. With the way the counter was situated, all it would take was for her customer to glance out of the door and make some kind of comment. With my luck, the middle-aged woman on holiday from one of the flyover states was nursing a *Fifty Shades of Grey* obsession, like most of the rest of her demographic. She'd see me walking blindfolded down the sidewalk and assume it was some kind of sex game and I'd have to find a new place to get my sugared pecan fix.

I shook my head and blew out a breath because it *was* some kind of sex game. The most frustrating one I'd ever played and apparently one with no actual sex involved. That should be a relief. It wasn't.

"What exactly are you trying to prove?" I turned my head and snapped the words in Jensen's direction, my patience frayed through its last thread.

The motion, combined with my anger, lack of sight, and four-inch heels, was enough to tip me off-balance. I wouldn't have fallen. I lived in heels. Balance was my middle name. I didn't get a chance to prove it. Jensen gripped my arms through the fabric of his suit coat and held me in place for a moment, steadying me. *The bastard.*

"Easy, kitten." He stepped into me until I could feel his body along the length of my back and his breath warm against the sensitive skin behind my ear.

"Kitten?" I snarled the word, too furious with the arrogant ass invading my personal space to care about who else might see us anymore. It was the second time he'd used the word and this time I was angry enough to set him straight. "Do you honestly think I'm some kind of helpless pet?"

I arched my back, pressing my butt against him, and was rewarded with the feel of his cock, rock hard and wedged against the seam of my ass. His hands slid down my arms to grip my hips, his fingers digging into my skin hard enough to leave marks. I spun in his arms, stretching up until I felt his breath against my lips. *Helpless, my ass.* I didn't have to see him to know exactly how hard he fought for control. His mouth might lie but I made my living reading people's body language. There was no puzzle hidden in the way his body reacted to mine.

"That's what I thought." I pitched my voice low, determined to do a better job than he had at hiding my body's reaction to being this close. I'd never been more grateful for having the less obvious genitals in my life. Of course, the trade-off was consistent, easily obtained orgasms, so maybe it wasn't a great deal, but at this point, I'd take my victories where I could get them.

Operating on the assumption that a strong offense made the best defense, I stretched up on my toes until my lips brushed his. I felt his breath rush out and took the opportunity to deepen the kiss until I felt his grip on my hips relax as he slid his hands around to cup my ass. Then I bit him. Hard. Dragging his bottom lip between my teeth, I tasted the metallic tang of blood.

In my head, the move would make him push me away and give me a bullshit excuse to rip the fucking tie off my eyes. In reality, he grabbed me tighter, lifting me off the ground and moving us quickly to the side. Before I got my bearings, he spun us until my back slammed up against the wall. The scrape of what felt like brick rubbed against my back through the fabric of his coat. At least he ruined his coat and not my Joie silk blouse. Then his hands gripped the back of my thighs, spreading me open and fitting himself against me, and I forgot about fabric and getting even and everything but the feel of the man in front of me.

He pressed the long, hard length of his cock into the damp silk of my panties and my stupid traitorous hips rocked against him, moving until he hit the spot I needed him most. He ate from my lips, kissing me like he was fucking me, his tongue giving me no option but to surrender to him. I met him, tasting and taking what I needed from him, riding the hard ridge of his erection as my body wound tighter. His hands slid from my thighs to my hips, pinning me against the wall as he broke the kiss and took a step back. I didn't have any choice but to let him go. It was either that or look like a needy fool and lose any scrap of power I might be able to salvage. It didn't stop my lips from trying to follow his, but I managed to pull myself together before I did something stupid like whimper.

"Are you going to safeword, Alexandra?" The ragged edge to his voice was some consolation, but not much considering how far my plan had gone off the rails.

"No." No way in hell was I admitting defeat. *Smug bastard.*

"Good," he said, twining his fingers with mine and tugging me forward a few steps as I scrambled to steady myself on my heels.

Next time we went on one of these blind walkabouts, I was wearing ballet flats. Like there was ever going to be a next time. Except even as I had the thought, I remembered the way my body reacted to him and knew if he asked me, I'd come up with some bat shit crazy way to justify doing it all again.

"We're here," he said, stopping so suddenly I had to tighten my grip on his hand to keep from stumbling.

I had no idea where *here* was. I was pretty sure we were in one of the alleyways off the Rue du Dauphine but with all the kissing and manhandling, I couldn't say for sure which way we'd turned. There was the sound of a door opening and a woman's soft voice said *bon jour,* as if seeing a man standing with a blindfolded woman in her doorway was an everyday occurrence. *Where the fuck were we?* I racked my brain, searching for anything familiar that might fit the input from my limited senses, but nothing clicked.

The room was cool but not air-conditioner cold and had the light scent of jasmine layered over the almost earthy scent the oldest homes in the Quarter never lost from too many years spent standing at or below sea level. It was quiet but not silent, as if there was something going on just outside where we stood. Before I could pinpoint anything else, Jensen gripped my elbow, squeezing gently, and led me across the room.

"Threshold." He murmured the word against my ear, lacing it with the kind of heat usually reserved for words like *nipple* or *pussy*.

I was so screwed. I'd spent five years of graduate and post-graduate school immersing myself in gender studies and the anti-feminist bias. I'd done my fucking thesis on the pervasive role of gender inequality in most aspects of everyday life, and here I was, letting some self-proclaimed Dom lead me around blindfolded. I didn't even have the threat of the lawsuit to use to justify my behavior. If anything, spending time with the attorney after he'd recused himself was more likely to hurt my case than help it. I'd clearly lost whatever good sense I may have initially possessed.

With my free hand, I reached for the tie knotted around my head, pausing when my fingertips brushed the cool silk. There wasn't a thing stopping me from taking off the blindfold and stopping this charade. The only thing stilling my hand was the knowledge—one I wasn't quite ready to admit to—that I felt something with Erik and his games. Something I'd never felt before. I'd gotten so used to trading my sexuality for power, to looking at everything as some kind of transaction or teaching moment. I couldn't remember the last time I'd given myself over to the pure sensation of an experience. I don't think I'd ever done it. Not really.

The realization made me a little sad and stopped me from tearing off the silk tie. They say curiosity killed the cat, which always struck me as a stupid phrase. Almost everything good that's ever happened in the world started because of someone's curiosity. They wanted to find an easier way to do something or wondered what would happen if. I wanted to find out what would happen if I went a little further. Surrendered just a bit more to this game we were playing.

"*Regarde ou vous marchez,*" said the woman's voice.

I dusted off my college French and wondered if she was telling Erik to watch his step or if her words were for me. His hand on my elbow was a steady presence, and I knew that whatever else might happen, he wouldn't let me fall. Which was weird because I'd *known* the man for all of an hour and we hadn't exactly started out as friends. None of that changed my certainty in at least this part of my relationship with him.

I sensed the walls closing in on us, and Erik shifted his body behind me, presumably so I could walk through another doorway. The sound of water splashing over something filled the background and the air changed from cool and dry to something warmer, more humid. Somehow more alive. I breathed in the scent of jasmine, stronger than before, closer. The floor had changed from the dull tap of wood underfoot to the click of masonry or stone. I heard the scrape of what could be a chair being pulled across a brick floor and then Erik gently urged me to sit.

"*L'apres-midi pour deux, s'il vous plait,*" he said in better French than I'd ever heard in college.

"*Oui, monsieur.*"

Erik's French extravaganza made it seem as if we were in a restaurant, but aside from the woman who met us at the door, I hadn't heard anyone else. Surely if there was someone else in the room with us, they would at least be whispering about the blindfolded woman. *Unless that kind of thing was the norm for this place.* In which case, where the hell had he brought me? I strained to hear anything that might give me a clue to my surroundings, but there was nothing other than the soft sound of splashing water.

I'd expected Erik to sit across from me so he could watch me and maybe gloat a little, but he pulled his chair up beside mine. He didn't crowd me—not exactly, but there was no way to ignore his presence or the way his body dwarfed mine. Not when he was this close. Hell, probably not even across the room.

"Where are we?" *May as well try the direct approach.* Not that I expected him to answer, but I'd already apparently decided to go along with this thing and not give him the satisfaction of safewording out. I was going to give myself a headache trying to figure out where we were on my own.

"It's a private club. You don't have to worry about being seen. Discretion is a condition of membership."

Well, that was a whole lot more words strung together than I expected, none of which made me feel any better about the situation. Except maybe the discretion thing, that part was good, but what kind of private club was within walking distance of my studio? I'd never seen anything that would have given me an indication that kind of place existed. Of course, that probably made sense. Hang a sign out and there was sure to be tourists wandering in off the street to ask about ghosts, voodoo rituals, or red rooms. New Orleans was a city of excess and flexible limits. Part of the reason people visited the Big Easy was to give in to her temptations and temporarily lose their minds.

"You're thinking so hard; you're going to give yourself a headache. Stop it."

I hated that his words mirrored my thoughts, and I hated it even more when people told me to stop thinking, like using your mind was somehow a bad thing. The whole rise of the anti-intellectual thing wore on my every last nerve. Since when did being smart become a negative instead of something to strive for? But regardless of what I thought about lawyers in general, you didn't get to be an attorney unless you were moderately intelligent. Erik didn't strike me as someone who was *moderately* anything. I could almost hear the smile in his voice, and found my thoughts drifting to the way his lips curved when he smiled. The way his face softened the few times he smiled at me, back before he knew my name.

He'd been different before he found out who I was. That didn't sit well. Neither did the idea that something I'd said or done had led to another person being hurt. My thoughts shifted to Kyle, the man who Erik said had hurt his partner. When we'd worked together, Kyle had been so timid. I'd had almost as hard of a time getting him to open up as I had with Peter. The idea of him taking things too far seemed impossible. Erik had to have it wrong. I opened my mouth to ask him for more information and closed it again when I heard someone approaching the table.

There was a rattle of china and someone set something in front of us. I breathed in and smelled the chicory-laced aroma of good coffee along with hot fat and melting powdered sugar. My mouth watered in response. *Beignets.* I'd bet money on it. There were lots of things that were oversold to lure in the tourists—stuffed baby alligators, gris-gris bags made in China—but the deep-fried pillows of dough covered in clouds of powdered sugar weren't one of them.

"Open your mouth, Alexandra."

For a fraction of a section, I thought he meant for me to ask my question, then I realized he planned to feed me like I was some kind of baby bird. *Oh for fuck's sake.* I rolled my eyes behind the blindfold. He was rocking moves out of some kind of bad knock-off of *9 ½ Weeks.* Except even as I wrapped myself in the condescension, I felt my body tighten and heat pool low in my belly. My mind might think he was ridiculous but my lady parts were more than ready to follow him wherever he led.

Telling myself it was the fastest way to get to the beignets, I opened my mouth and waited. I heard him suck in a breath and flashed to an image of what I must look like to him. At his mercy, blindfolded, with my mouth open, waiting for him to fill it. The image shifted to me on my knees, my ponytail wrapped around his fist while he teased my bottom lip with his thick, hard cock. I felt my face flush and wondered if we were thinking the same thing, which only made my cheeks hotter.

The powdered sugar hit my tongue a fraction of a second before the warm fried dough short-circuited the pathway of rational thought to my brain. I let out a groan of pleasure and heard Erik's deep throaty chuckle beside me, warming me from the inside out.

"Bite, Alexandra. We both know how much you like to do that."

ERIK

FUCK ME. I WATCHED THE powdered sugar land on her waiting tongue and all I could think about was what it would be like if it was drops of my cum instead of sugar painting her sweet lips. My reaction to this woman threatened to knock me completely sideways. I ran my tongue over my bottom lip, exacerbating the slight sting from her bite.

I'd intended to make it through the rest of our time together without touching her for anything other than to keep her from falling. She'd completely shot that plan to hell, backing her ass up against me and trying to top from the bottom. I was supposed to leave her wanting—begging me to touch her. Instead, I'd pushed her up against the wall and had her legs wrapped around my hips before I thought things through.

I couldn't remember the last time I'd lost control like that. Scratch that; I could. It was with her earlier in the day when I'd gone on my professional self-destructive spree and recused myself from the case I'd brought into the firm. I wasn't done feeling the pain from that. I still had to explain it to Jared and the other partners. There wasn't an excuse I could give that my friend wouldn't see through. It didn't matter. I held the beignet to Alexandra's lips, told her to bite and watched her sharp white teeth sink into the pastry. Given the choice, I'd do the same thing all over again. But this time I'd be ready for her when she wielded her sexuality like a finely-honed sword, and she'd never get a chance to draw first blood.

Everything about her railed against giving in to being fed. I could read her conflict in the set of her shoulders and the tilt of her head. In the way her pulse beat against the slender column of her pale throat. She hated the idea of surrendering, of letting me take care of her, but she wanted it too. I imagined the conflict going on in her head was as voracious as the one I was experiencing.

Whether she'd admit it to herself or not, she'd submitted beautifully, with a lot less argument than I'd expected. If you ignored the biting, which was hard to ignore. I shifted in my chair, giving my perpetually hard cock more room. I'd started to feel like one of those four-hour warnings on erectile dysfunction commercials. I'd been hard since halfway through the deposition, and it showed every sign of getting worse before it got better. Watching Alexandra take the first tentative steps across her studio and then later out onto Saint Charles, seeing the way she braved something she was unsure of—the way she trusted me to keep her safe—made me want to push every boundary she had and see how far she'd let us take things. And it made me want her more than was rational.

"Any chance you ordered coffee?" she said, licking the powdered sugar from her lips.

Feeding her wasn't going the way I'd hoped. Her cheeks were flushed, and I'd bet more money than I paid for this session with her that her nipples were hard. And her pussy wet. She wanted this—wanted me—but she'd laced her tone with enough bored indulgence to tell me she wasn't focused on the sensations around her, not completely. If she spent too much time in that gorgeous head of hers, I'd lose whatever temporary advantage I'd managed to gain.

I weighed my options. She'd play along with eating out of my hand because regardless of what I still had to learn about Dr. Smithson, I knew without a doubt, she didn't lose. Not if she could help it. We had that in common. For now, she saw her submission as a kind of winning—a false kind maybe and not the kind I hoped she would by the time we were finished, but enough that she'd play along and not feel anything genuine. I already knew she had no problem shedding her clothes and precious little trouble with public displays of intimacy. The ones that had nothing to do with genuine intimacy.

I could get her to slip her panties off under the table, maybe even bring her to the edge of orgasm with my hand, but I doubted if any of that would make her feel truly vulnerable. Sex was a currency she traded in. I wanted more. And despite my better judgment, I found myself wanting to look into her eyes, to watch her react to the beauty around us.

"Hello? Coffee?"

"It's sitting in front of you."

The crease in her forehead deepened, and she blew out a breath, clearly frustrated. When she slid her hand carefully over the linen-covered table, I caught her fingertips, stopping her.

"Let me guess. You want to hold the cup."

Brat. I didn't give a fuck about the cup. I wanted to take care of her. To offer her something from my hand and have her take it willingly. Eagerly. I wanted something real.

"Take off my tie."

I felt her fingers stiffen against my palm as if I'd asked her to strip naked. She pulled free of my hand and reached for the blindfold, pausing when her fingertips brushed the silk.

"This isn't the same as safewording, right? I'm not giving up?"

She acted as if she was concerned about losing a bet. She may as well have said *giving in. Surrendering. Losing.* I could tell she thought they were all the same thing. The realization made me sad, which was its own special kind of fucked up.

"No, kitten, you're not *safewording.* Not unless you want to."

She shook her head and then made quick work of the knot at the back of her head. When she pulled the silk away from her eyes, she blinked, her eyes going wide as she took in our surroundings.

"This is lovely," she said, her voice taking on a slightly breathless quality that made me want to find other ways to steal her breath.

Given her line of work—or perhaps because of it—she seemed out of touch with her desire. She wielded her sexuality with a cutting precision that left little room for simple sensual pleasure. With the exception of the rush that came from holding power, I wasn't sure her pleasure had any place at all in the way she experienced sex. Wanting to change that bumped itself to the top of my list of priorities. She might appear experienced to the point of being jaded but I had a feeling when it came to honestly experiencing genuine pleasure, Alexandra was a virgin. I wanted to be the one to share it with her.

We were seated at a small garden table in one of the private alcoves. We were the only ones in the open air courtyard but it wouldn't have mattered if we weren't. Only members and their guests had access to the space and no one who made it past the front door would talk about what happened on the other side. Madame Arlene's was a hidden gem with a very exclusive clientele: my partners at the firm and the club, a few local politicians, and the occasional business leader. Membership was invitation only and had more to do with discretion and power than personal wealth, although I doubted anyone without considerable means had ever been offered a spot.

The club didn't offer anything a five-star hotel wouldn't. In addition to the café we were sitting in, there were a few smaller rooms that could be converted to private dining rooms and a handful of lavishly appointed guest suites upstairs. What Madame Arlene provided was much more valuable than superior service and luxury. She gave members a place to meet with whoever they wanted—no questions asked, no possibility of the press stealing a photograph. For some, it was a place to have clandestine meetings with mistresses or for the few women members, the male equivalent, without leaving a pesky paper trail the divorce attorneys could find.

For me, it had been a place to bring submissives, where we could push boundaries outside places like Bacchus without risking either of us being exposed in a way we didn't want. I hadn't brought a submissive to

Arlene's since Julie. Bringing Alexandra was a bigger step than I'd expected to take with her that day—hell, ever. My initial intention had been to show her all the many ways she'd fucked up, give her a taste of real submission and go back to my regular life while someone else at my firm finished the lawsuit, and I finished thinking about the arrogant woman who thought she could teach something she didn't believe in.

After I got a taste of her, that all changed. I found myself wanting more time. She followed my orders without questioning but she did it because she wanted to best me, not out of any kind of partnership. I knew it was crazy to expect it from her or to even want it. She hadn't come to me willingly. Why should I expect her to act like she had? I hadn't had that kind of genuine intimacy, the kind of power exchange that felt like my partner and I were performing a duet or making a beautiful piece of art together since Julie, and we'd been together for three years before our relationship ended. Even then, the fluidity of that kind of relationship had been intermittent. I'd known Alexandra for a sum total of a couple of hours. It didn't stop me from wanting that kind of intimacy with her. Which meant I was well and truly fucked, because the one thing I was fairly sure Dr. Smithson didn't do was intimacy.

Like many of the private courtyards in the city, the small space held a gazing pool with a small bubbling fountain. Jasmine climbed the brick wall on one side, perfuming the air and adding to the sense of barely restrained wildness, while verbena and other herbs fought for space in the small planting areas carved out between the cobblestone pavers. It was a lush, humid oasis and an exercise in barely restrained excess. The perfect place to bring the woman who seemed determined to keep her desires under lock and key.

"I had no idea this place existed," she said, glancing around the room.

"It's not open to the public."

She arched a brow in question as she sipped her café au lait.

"Members and guests only. Discretion is paramount. I was confident that was something you could both appreciate and respect." Despite my earlier lapses in judgment, I wouldn't have brought her to Madame Arlene's if I'd had any question about her ability to keep a secret. Her livelihood depended on maintaining others' privacy.

She tipped her cup in mock salute before reaching across to snag a beignet from the plate sitting in front of me. The simple act illustrated how little she cared about impressing me. Normally, I'd correct her and serve her myself either from my plate or my hand but coaxing Alexandra out of her shell was going to be more challenging than making friends with a reluctant hermit crab. I didn't want to bash through her shell; I wanted her to come to me willingly.

She bit into the pastry and let out a groan of pure pleasure that made anything else I'd been thinking irrelevant. That sound—the sound of her surrendering to the shear sensual pleasure of an experience—became my new Holy Grail.

"These are better than the beignets at the Café du Monde—different somehow," she said, taking another bite and letting her eyes drift closed.

When she licked the powdered sugar from her lips, it was because she wanted the taste, not with any kind of artifice designed to seduce. It was for her pleasure alone, which had what I was sure was the unintended consequence of amplifying mine.

"They infuse the water they use to make the dough with herbs."

She looked at me as if I'd just spoken Greek. Reaching over, I ran my thumb over the crease in her forehead, smoothing her pale skin. Her gaze stayed locked on mine, her brown eyes slightly wary, and I felt the way her breath hitched at my touch. I wanted her on edge, unable to hide behind her normal carefully constructed walls. The easiest way to do that seemed to be sneaking in gentle touches when she was preoccupied with something else and couldn't slip into her practiced routine. I gave myself the pleasure of sliding my hand down to cup her cheek for a moment before letting go of her and relaxing back in my chair. She leaned forward at the absence of my touch and I felt a small flash of triumph. Not a victory— not yet—in the war or even the battle, but all parties were present on the field.

"You know how they make the beignets?" The crease was back in place on her forehead but this time I stayed my hand.

"I like to cook. I could arrange for them to show you if you want, or I could teach you myself." As soon as the words left my mouth, I knew it would be the latter. Before we were done with each other, I'd have Alexandra in my kitchen, eating out of my hand not because of some dare, but because that's exactly where she wanted to be.

"I don't cook. This is New Orleans. People come here to eat. Why would I think I could make anything better than what I can get from one of the over a thousand restaurants?"

I tipped my head to the side, watching her for a moment. "For the pleasure of creating something yourself."

She looked so genuinely puzzled at what I'd said, I left the rest of what I'd been thinking trail off and picked up a beignet instead. They'd cooled and the powdered sugar had melted into the fat, making almost a sweet pasty icing on the surface of the pillow of dough, but even cold, Arlene's beignets were the best I'd ever tasted.

"Would you like a fresh batch?" I asked when she'd finished the last pastry.

"No," she said, looking at the empty plate with longing. "I think I'm always going to want more of those, but I'm full."

I loved the way she'd eaten without reservation, and I got the sense that she was saying no because she was genuinely sated and not out of some misguided attempt to deny herself. Some women had strange relationships with food, but that seemed like the easiest way to get behind Alexandra's walls. She appeared, for the moment at least, comfortable enjoying the pleasure of eating with me, or perhaps in spite of me. If I'd been someone she cared about impressing, maybe she would have acted differently. It didn't matter what the reason was. I'd found the seam in the oyster shell and I intended to work at it until I pried it open, revealing the pearl inside.

She took a swallow of her coffee and I watched her hesitate a moment as she set the thin china cup back in its saucer.

"Can I ask you something?"

"Anything," I said. I might not answer, but I wanted her to ask.

"Can you tell me more about what happened with Kyle? At the club you mentioned?"

I felt my jaw tighten at the unwanted image of the middle-aged man being forcibly escorted from Bacchus. But he was the reason I'd ended up neck-deep in the clusterfuck of a lawsuit and the reason Alexandra was sitting next to me.

"He was so timid during our sessions," she said, filling the space when I didn't immediately answer. It might have been nerves but it felt more like a genuine desire to understand what had gone wrong.

"He beat his submissive with a cane, hard enough to break the skin. If the dungeon monitor hadn't stopped him, he would have permanently marked her."

She gasped and covered her mouth with her hands. The shock and horror was clear in her eyes. Part of me wanted to take that away from her—to give her a beautiful image to replace it. The other part wanted to show her the photographs the club had taken to document the injuries in case anything further came of the encounter. I settled someplace in between, waiting for her to deal with the reality of the situation. She'd been playing with power she didn't fully understand and innocence was no excuse. Not when people got hurt.

"I don't understand," she said, curling in on herself.

"I know. That's part of the problem."

I took a sip of my coffee, letting the silence stretch between us for a moment. I didn't know her well, but I understood Dr. Smithson enough to know that her intentions were good, if misguided. If she believed she'd done something wrong, she'd chastise herself for it. She wouldn't need me to punish her. Not for that.

"Tell me why you started the Gentleman's Submissive. Why not teach or go back and get your counselor's license? Go into private practice?"

"I thought I could help people."

I bit back a snort of disbelief.

"I know. The irony's not lost on me," she said, holding a hand up in front of her and suddenly looking very tired.

I took her hand, cradling her slender fingers in my palm while I gently cuffed her wrist with my other hand. I wanted her to feel safe with me. Safe enough to tell me the truth.

"I wanted to be a professor—write a book about the consequences of the shifting power dynamics between the sexes. Something like that."

She'd gone from seeming like a confident academic to sounding lost, and I stroked her wrist, feeling her pulse beat against my thumb. The desire to protect her, to soothe her had moved in and set up housekeeping in my psyche, and I had no doubt it would come back to bite me in the ass.

"Why didn't you?"

"There aren't a lot of professorships in gender studies. Turns out the people in the jobs have no intentions of going anywhere. Classic supply and demand."

She looked thoughtful and I waited for a moment, giving her space to work through whatever was going on in that gorgeous head of hers.

"I think I wanted to be more hands-on. Don't laugh," she said, the smile lighting her up from the inside.

"Wouldn't dream of it."

"Bullshit." She paused for a moment, as if deciding how much to share. "I grew up reading Harlequin bodice rippers under the soapstone counter in chem lab and then sneaking my hand into my panties in the bathroom between classes."

"Please God, tell me you went to a Catholic school." Images of Alexandra in plaid skirts and knee socks filled my head. I added *play professor and naughty schoolgirl* to the to-do list I'd started to compile. I'd have to see if I could dig up a wooden ruler from somewhere.

"Sorry, dirty old man, but no."

I hit her with my best Big Bad Wolf grin and waited until she couldn't help but smile in return.

"The point I was trying to make before you got all skeezy."

I snorted. I hadn't pegged Dr. Smithson as someone who'd use that word.

"The point is," she repeated, ignoring my laughter, "I knew the books had something I wanted—a fantasy of being taken and made to feel things. I just had no idea what that meant or how to reconcile it with the other things I knew to be true about myself. And I'm not the only one." She took a swallow of her coffee and I waited, curious to see where she'd take us. "Women want to rule the world and lots of them want to be dominated by the bad boy in the bedroom. Traditional roles for women are the exception, not the norm, anymore and the world is a better place for it. I'm not going to say *we have to* or *we're expected to* succeed in meaningful careers because for most of us work is an important part of our identities, not something we do because someone else tells us to. Women are badass powerhouses. So how is a woman who kicks ass in the boardroom supposed to reconcile that with wanting the man she loves to spank her?"

She was slipping back into the persona she'd had at the deposition, but it felt genuine this time. She telling her truth and she'd clearly spent a lot of time thinking about it. If she ever got the chance, she'd make a damn fine professor.

"And it's not easier for men," she said, sitting forward in the chair as if the idea excited her. "How are they supposed to reconcile the alpha asshole thing with being the guy who picks up the kids from daycare?"

She was right. I'd known from the first moment I'd started thinking about sex that I was dominant and even I didn't understand the full spectrum of BDSM, from a little light tie me up/tie me down to the master/slave arrangement and everything in between. I'd simply accepted that everyone had their own kink comfort zone and beyond safe, sane, and consensual, I didn't have to have an opinion.

I watched as her expression shifted from excitement to something else, something sadder.

"I'm so sorry about what happened with Kyle. I wanted to help him find his confidence. I never meant for anyone to get hurt."

Things would have been different if her response held any of the arrogance or posturing of our initial encounter. I might not have fallen if I hadn't seen the honest remorse in her eyes.

"The sub he worked with would have been hard for an experienced Dom to handle. She was, for lack of a better word, a pain slut." I hated the phrase, but in this case it fit. My firm did legal work for Bacchus. I'd reviewed the tape myself, trying to decide how to handle the potential liability. All the players signed a disclaimer but that didn't mean someone wouldn't try to sue. The sub had never given any indication of wanting to use her safe word, and I didn't believe it was a case of her forgetting. "She pushed him harder than either of them should have gone. A more experienced Dom would have known how to set limits even while she seemed intent on pushing past them."

"I guess that makes sense," she said, looking like it was a very small comfort.

"Not knowing doesn't make the guy a bad person, but it doesn't absolve him either. And it doesn't make him any less dangerous. The problem, or one of the problems, is that because of his time with you, Kyle thought he *was* trained. He believed he knew more than he did, and it made him take risks he wouldn't have otherwise."

I felt conflicted about the direction our afternoon had taken. Being able to talk to her about what she'd been doing wrong and more importantly having her hear and understand it gave me an enormous sense of satisfaction, but I hated seeing the way her thoughts had turned in on themselves. She'd slipped out of the present in the courtyard with me and back into the spiral of her work and the past. That didn't work for me.

"Our time's not up yet." I pinned her with my gaze until she had no choice but to look up at me. "We can talk more later if you want, but right now I want to get back to where we were."

Her lips curved in what might have been a grateful smile and she nodded. As I watched, she drew in a shaky breath and her chest rose under the fabric of my suit coat.

"Take off my jacket."

It was comfortable in the courtyard, not the normal muggy heat of early September. The shade and fountain kept it from ever feeling like the oven the rest of the city could feel like, but it wasn't so cool she needed the jacket and I wanted to see her nipples through the silk of her blouse.

"I thought you wanted me to feel it move over my breasts and imagine your hands on me?"

I loved the fact that she remembered that part of my instructions ahead of the part about not letting anyone else see her. And I loved that she was so eager to move past our conversation and meet me back in the present.

"Pretend my gaze is the same as my touch. We both know you're good at pretending and I want to see the way your nipples tighten underneath the silk."

She slipped the jacket off with a practiced ease that let me know we were heading back into familiar territory for her. I swear this woman took her clothes off the same way other women put them on, with no sense of false modesty at all. She turned to put the jacket on the back of her chair and I took it from her, draping it across my lap and my thickening cock. Fuck, everything she did made me hard for her.

I would be the one to put the jacket back on her when we were ready to leave. Catching and holding her defiant gaze for a moment, I saw her shift so she sat straighter in her chair, shoulders back and spine bowed slightly to press her breasts toward me. Taking my time, I let my gaze follow the curve of her jaw, down the slender column of her throat to pause at the place her heart beat hard under her pale skin. She slid halfway back into her sex kitten persona, but her body gave her away. The hammering of her pulse meant she wasn't as immune to this as she might pretend.

My gaze followed the line of her collarbone, peeking out from the open neckline of her blouse. I couldn't wait to run my tongue along the same path my gaze took, and I didn't bother trying to hide my desire from her. I couldn't expect honesty from her if I didn't offer it up myself—at least in part. I wanted her. It would be foolish to try to hide it.

The swell of her breasts and the dip between was just visible at the edge of her blouse. Sometime very soon I was going to hang a rough-cut diamond around her neck and watch the way it flashed against her gorgeous flesh. Her already hard nipples tightened to points under my gaze. I'd put diamonds there as well. Small jewels on chains that I could cinch around the tips of her swollen nipples. She'd wear them until her breasts ached with the pleasure of the bite of pain and then I'd take them off with my teeth, suckling her abused flesh until I got her to come with nothing more than my mouth.

"Fuck." She breathed out the word, more of a prayer than a curse, and I wondered for a second if I'd spoken aloud.

It was my turn to arch a brow at her. Her dark eyes had dilated to almost black and her cheeks flushed a pretty rose color. I wondered if the rest of her skin would flush as easily, and my cock throbbed at the idea.

"The way you look at me. As if I'm treasure and you're some kind of pirate." She let the rest of the thought trail off and her posture slipped from posing to something that managed to be both more relaxed and somehow more vulnerable at the same time.

"You're beautiful, Alexandra. Your body and your mind. You're meant to be savored." I let the words carry the certainty I felt. I didn't doubt she was used to being desired, but I had a feeling honest appreciation was another thing entirely. I didn't have any trouble giving her that.

Ignoring my aching cock, throbbing in time with the beat of my heart, I watched her for a few moments longer, like a diabetic with his face pressed against the window of a candy shop. I intended to look my fill, but I wouldn't touch her again. Not yet. Not until she begged me for it and only then if I was sure she was really ready.

Every breath she took drew the silk across her tight nipples and I imagined what it must feel like to her. What it would feel like for me to put my mouth on her and suckle her through the silk. Watching her shallow breaths, I tortured us both by keeping her on edge and denying myself what I wanted from her. When she squirmed in her chair, shifting to press her thighs together to relieve some of the ache, I didn't bother to hide my grin.

Alex

WE'D GONE FROM THE WEIRD baby bird thing to talking about Kyle and finally ended up with me wriggling in my chair, so close to coming I was sure a single brush of my clit would set me off. I couldn't get my bearings around Erik. Every time I thought I knew where we were going, he changed directions on me. It was maddening. And almost as delicious as the beignets.

Any relief I felt at finding out what happened with Kyle was mitigated by the fact that the whole thing was my fault in the first place. I hadn't wielded the cane but I'd given him permission to do it, permission he'd never have accepted without my prompting him. I was going to unpack all of that later. I hadn't been lying when I told Erik I started the Gentleman's Submissive to help people, not hurt them. If there was a better—safer—way to do my job, I'd take the new information and adjust. For now I was going to concentrate on trying not to come, sitting in the chair next to the too sure of himself attorney.

"Do you usually orgasm during your sessions, Alexandra?"

Well, fuck. I sucked in a breath and tried to figure out how to parse my answer while blood my brain needed headed to my lady parts.

"No, not usually," I said, careful to keep my words as neutral as possible. Talking to Erik about orgasms was a bit like Red Riding Hood dancing through an arena with a revved-up bull. The last thing I wanted to do was throw down the orgasm gauntlet. He sure as hell didn't need to know how close I was just from his words. From the way his gaze traveled over my body. Hell, even from the way he'd fed me with his hand. "It's easier for me to do my job if I keep my physical responses out of it."

The truth was I almost never came with anyone else around. I had a pretty extensive collection of vibrators—business expense (*take that, IRS*)—and I knew my body. I orgasmed regularly; it was just usually a solo affair. I liked it that way. It was easier for me to relax and enjoy myself when I wasn't worried about what the guy was thinking or feeling, assuming they put their attention in the right place to begin with. I had a feeling Erik knew exactly where to focus his attention. *Sexy bastard.*

"What a shame," he said, sounding like he meant the exact opposite. "Are you ready?" He stood without waiting for my response and held out his jacket for me to slip into.

"Sure. Yes, thank you," I said, wary of the turn our afternoon had taken.

I stretched my arms out to put on his jacket and felt the silk slide over my aching nipples. They were hard enough to use as engraving tools and showed absolutely no sign of changing. Not unless Erik decided to take mercy on me and suck them into submission. The thought of his mouth, hot and wet, tugging on my silk-covered nipple was enough to make my knees give way and I had to reach for the back of the chair to steady myself. I tugged his jacket tighter around me before I did something crazy—like tear open my blouse and offer myself to him.

"I can find my way back from here," I said, knowing before I said the words that he'd never let me off that easy. "I'll message your jacket back to you."

"I'm walking you back," he said, his grin almost predatory.

"Of course you are," I said, turning toward the doorway we must have entered through. I heard his chuckle, a warm, deep rumble behind me. *Fuck, even his laughter turned me on.*

I didn't give him a chance to blindfold me again, although I didn't doubt he'd insist if that's what he really wanted. He didn't strike me as the kind of man who had any trouble getting what he wanted. As I started across the courtyard, I felt his hand, a warm and solid presence on the small of my back, guiding me even when I no longer needed him to. I murmured my thanks to the stunning coffee-colored woman who carried herself with the grace and bearing of the granddaughter of a voodoo priestess. I wasn't often self-conscious but it would be hard for any woman to stand next to the breathtaking woman and not feel like the ugly stepsister.

Erik leaned in to brush a kiss over the woman's cheek. He murmured something in her ear, and she replied softly, too low and fast for my high school French to translate. Something tightened deep in my chest. If I looked closely at my emotions, I'd have guessed it was misplaced jealousy. *Good thing I wasn't looking closely.* At my feelings anyway. I concentrated my attention on the elegant room I'd missed when I walked through it blindfolded. The windows were shuttered against the afternoon heat and partially, I imagined, to preserve the elegant furnishings. There were new pieces but I'd bet money I didn't have that the furnishings that looked like antiques were original. The place whispered old money in a mixture of soft Southern drawl and French Creole.

Erik held the door for me and followed me outside. I recognized our location on the edge of the Quarter. I must have walked by the spot dozens of times and never noticed anything more than a tidy stucco exterior with green-black railings and shutters. Somehow knowing the courtyard was hidden from people walking past made it feel even more special. Like a secret we shared. Except it wasn't; he'd obviously been there lots of times, presumably with many different women. *Which didn't matter, because it wasn't like we were a couple or anything.* Hell, at the beginning of the day, we hadn't even liked each other.

That part, at least, seemed to have changed.

Aside from the fact that I liked it much better when random people didn't hate my guts, it might mean that I wouldn't lose everything after all. Of course, given my new perspective, I wasn't sure exactly how I was going to handle things with the Gentleman's Submissive moving forward, but I'd figure all of that out.

"So you're really completely off the case?"

"Yes, Alexandra," he said, shocking the hell out of me by taking my hand in his.

He laced our fingers together like we were on some kind of date. Like we were a couple. I was pretty sure one of his goals was making sure I stayed as off-balance as possible. Every time I got my bearings, he tilted things again.

"So what happens with the case?" I might have gone way off script where Jensen was concerned. My nipples and clit seemed firmly in his camp, but I still had a business to run and student loans to pay back. And I wouldn't mind having enough money left over to buy myself some of those beignets again. *Maybe there was some kind of black market for the delicious pillows of tarragon-scented dough.*

"You're going to have to ask your attorney about that. It's better for both of us if we don't talk about it."

I glanced over at him, searching his profile to see if he was telling me the truth or feeding me convenient bullshit. There was the barest hint of stubble along his strong jaw and I got distracted imagining for a moment what it would feel like scraping against my inner thigh. The thought of beard burn made me inadvertently squeeze his fingers, and he glanced in my direction, giving me a smile when he caught me watching him. *Oh, for fuck's sake.* Clearly my body didn't need me for anything related to Erik. My lips curved in response to his and heat pooled low in my belly. Didn't matter, apparently, whether my mind thought it was a good idea; my body was all in where he was concerned. But I didn't think he was trying to bullshit me. At least not about the legal stuff. I'd take the rest on a case-by-case basis.

In a few minutes, we were standing in front of the door to the building that housed my studio, and I realized I had no idea what happened next. Did I give him his coat, tell him good-bye and never see him again? That idea didn't sit as well with me as I'd expected. I was still super shaky on the whole *I'm a Dom* thing. A little blindfold and café au lait wasn't enough to change my long-held beliefs that quickly. But I had to admit, I'd never felt anything like what Erik made me feel.

I'd never backed down from a challenge, although I was starting to have a harder time thinking about whatever we were doing in term of winners and losers anymore. I'd also never turned away from knowledge that could make me better at my job—better at anything. Whatever he might call himself, Erik knew things I didn't. I searched my head, trying to figure out a way to ask him to teach me without having to give up too much power in the process and drawing a blank.

"I want another session," he said, still holding my hand as we stood on the sidewalk in front of the door to my building.

I resisted the urge to do a mental touchdown dance.

"I charged you double," I said, still not sure how I'd ended up in this crazy place. I'd started my day terrified of the law and ended it aroused past the point of reason.

"I figured," he said with a laugh.

I liked it when he laughed. It was a rich, throaty sound, like burnt sugar or good Scotch. For a brief moment, when he laughed, he looked lighter somehow. Easier. It would be worth it to figure out how to make his face wear that expression.

He reached into his pocket with his free hand and pulled out his phone, swiping his finger across the screen a few times. I didn't need to hear it to know that somewhere up in my studio my phone was dinging with an incoming message.

"I sent payment for the next session—regular rate this time."

"I never said yes."

"Are you saying no?" He watched me, waiting.

"No. I mean yes." I felt my face heat and bit back a groan. The very last thing I wanted was for Erik to know how flustered he made me. I imagined he had a pretty good idea, but I didn't need to make it easier for him. "Another session would be okay."

He grinned at me and the pirate thing was back. All he needed was a cutlass strapped to his hip and a compass tattoo. Of course, for all I knew, he had a tattoo hidden somewhere underneath the polished cotton of his expensive dress shirt. Without thinking, I licked my lips and it was his turn to squeeze my hand.

"I'm going to save us both and go back to work," he said, bringing our joined hands to his lips and pressing his mouth to the delicate skin on the inside of my wrist.

Feeling my pulse hammer against his lips, he kept his gaze locked on me for a moment and I wondered whether he was reconsidering his earlier position. In favor of a position that had me bent over the spanking bench upstairs with him driving that long, thick cock I'd felt earlier inside me until I screamed his name and promised him anything his pirate heart desired.

"I need you to do something for me."

I nodded, an overwhelming cocktail of sexy hormones making me momentarily mute.

"You said you didn't orgasm with clients and with the cease-and-desist you won't be seeing anyone else this week anyway; sessions with me don't count," he hurried to add. "Until we have our next session, I don't want you to orgasm alone."

I didn't hold back my groan. I should have seen this coming. Orgasm denial was classic BDSM stuff. I should have known we'd end up here, but I'd wanted to believe so much that he was different than the *your orgasms belong to me* alphaholes I'd read about. I let my desire cloud my judgment. Like every other woman on the planet.

"Let me guess," I said, tugging my hand free of his and feeling the loss immediately. "You don't want me to orgasm without your permission." I slid enough derision in my voice to make it clear exactly what I thought about his suggestion.

"Good Lord, no," he said, laughing so loud a couple passing on the street glanced in our direction. "Kitten." He pitched his voice low and despite my frustration, I leaned closer. "I want you to have as many orgasms as you possibly can. I want your body drenched with sweat as you ride your hand or your vibrator—hell, the fucking bed frame for all I care. Spend all day, every day, figuring how to get yourself off if you want."

His words sent my already aroused body on hyper alert. My panties had gone from damp to drenched and were rapidly heading toward natural disaster state.

"But you said..." I stuttered the words out as soon as I managed to marshal enough breath to make a sound.

"I said I don't want you to orgasm alone. Before you come, you need to send me a text, call me, send me a video or a screaming voice mail. Just don't go it alone. Reach out."

I worked his instructions around in my head, trying them on for size. The idea of him listening to me climax both excited and terrified me. I'd never planned on letting him get that close, which was insane on any level because I'd stripped naked for the man. He was settling for something as anonymous as a text.

"Why?"

Before he answered, he reached out to cuff my wrist with his hand, circling it with his thumb and index finger, catching me in place and making me feel both small and safe.

"Part of submitting and real intimacy is a willingness to make yourself vulnerable. I have a feeling it's been a long time since you've been vulnerable with anyone."

I wanted to deny it, to tell him he was full of shit, but I couldn't lie to him. Not about this.

"Can you do that for me?"

I swallowed hard and nodded.

I managed to make it to the elevator and let the doors slide shut behind me before I slid my hand into my panties. My fingertips slipped effortlessly over my clit. I couldn't remember ever being this wet. Before the car reached the third floor, I was sagging against the wall, Erik's name on my lips as the orgasm crashed over me.

The first climax barely took the edge off my hunger and any satisfaction evaporated as the doors slid open on the floor to my studio. I was going to have to do that again, who knew how many times, to work the lawyer out of my system so I could concentrate on something other than the way he made my body respond. I ignored, for the time being, I'd promised to tell him when I did. I could probably lump them together. One text for a handful of orgasms should do it. I was going to sink into a long, hot bubble bath, come as many times as I wanted and call it one. One bath. One session. Letter of the law and all that shit.

I keyed in the code to the studio. I could have gone home and straight to the bath, but I needed my phone. And my bra. Without Erik's jacket, I felt much too exposed to walk the short distance to my apartment. Ignoring the way my body tightened at the memory of the last time I'd been in the space, I crossed the room. One of the drawers to my cabinet was open a fraction of an inch. I went to close it and then stopped, pulling it open instead. There was an empty space in the red velvet lining where one of the pairs of nipple clamps normally sat. *The man had pocketed my clamps.*

Ignoring the tingle in my breasts at the idea of Erik walking around with nipple clamps in his pocket, I closed the drawer. I made quick work of shrugging into my bra and refastening my blouse. When I was sure I was presentable, I grabbed my phone. Email would have to do. I'd never gotten his number. Except when I woke up my phone, there was a new stored contact. Under *Sir.*

It was marginally better than *Master*, I suppose.

CAME IN THE ELEVATOR. SORRY. DIDN'T HAVE MY PHONE.

I watched the screen, waiting for his reply. It came back so quickly he must have been expecting my text.

SINCE I KNOW HOW MUCH YOU WANTED ME, WE'LL MAKE AN EXCEPTION THIS TIME.

Well hell, I hadn't exactly thought that one through. The man didn't need any help with his confidence.

I WANT MY NIPPLE CLAMPS BACK. SURELY YOU MAKE ENOUGH TO BUY YOUR OWN.

It took longer for him to reply, and I was feeling a little smug for maybe finally leaving him speechless for a change.

KITTEN, THE NEXT TIME YOU SEE THEM, YOU'LL BE WEARING THEM.

I swallowed hard (I had a feeling it was going to replace my antacid habit), silenced my phone and locked up for the day. I didn't stand a chance.

ERIK

I FINISHED LISTENING TO THE text-to-voice app read back the last of the string of emails and popped the earbud out. I'd already gone over the notes for the meeting a dozen or so times. I should be ready, but after the debacle with the GS case, I couldn't afford to fuck this up. I'd messaged the other partners about my recusal and forwarded the files to one of the junior associates, but I'd taken the chicken-shit way out, disguised as business, and hadn't actually spoken to anyone. I had no idea the extent of the fallout, but it couldn't be good.

I'd been tightening the ropes around the shipping firm for months. Tonight was the night to close the deal and move my firm into the number-one spot as counsel for one of the largest transportation companies in the country. Hell, it was only a matter of time before they were number one in the world. If—when—I got them to sign with us, I'd be a superhero.

Assuming I didn't let the distraction get the better of me. Alex had me twisted up in knots. I'd spent way too much time trying to push her out of my head, with only marginal success. I tucked the notes into my folio. The words had started to turn and run into each other anyway.

I glanced down at my phone one last time to see if she'd responded to my last text. I hadn't heard from her since her elevator text and that was too damn long ago. I could multitask with the best of them, but only if I could compartmentalize the different pieces. The sexy Dr. Smithson managed to work her way into everything, and I was having a hard time picking out the individual threads, which wasn't going to work for me. I needed this dinner to go well.

The town car pulled to a stop in front of the restaurant and I tried to ignore the jolt I got from seeing the place where I caught Alex the first time we met. Maybe dinner at Matt's hadn't been such a great idea. I'd chosen it weeks ago because the staff knew me and would go out of their way to ensure the dinner went off without a hitch. As long as I managed to stay out of my own fucking way.

I thanked the driver and hurried through the front door. The pretty hostess smiled at me and led me to a table on the second floor overlooking the balcony, where Jared was already waiting, looking a thousand times more comfortable than I felt.

"You need to chill the fuck out, man," said Jared, after I'd placed my drink order and dropped my folio on the floor. "Clients can smell desperation a mile away. What's wrong with you?"

"Nothing. I'm fine." Or I would be by the time the Gulf Enterprises team arrived. I might have to work harder than Jared at some things, but confidence wasn't usually one of them.

"First you're dropping cases and now you're twitchy before meetings. Get it together."

That answered the question about whether he'd heard about the recusal and added to the long list of things I didn't want to talk about. I couldn't bullshit Jared. He might not figure out the truth but he'd smell the lie.

"Stop being an ass. The client's here." Grateful for the diversion, I stood as the hostess led the small group to our table. The fact that I thought of the reason for the meeting as a diversion illustrated how screwed-up my priorities had become.

I managed to make it through the small talk over appetizers and worked my way into the meat of the deal during the entrees. By the time the server set the blood orange-infused custards in front of us, I'd hit my stride. Jared had relaxed back into his chair, clearly confident in my ability to close.

"We'll take good care of you," I said, standing and clasping the owner's hand after the coffee cups were empty and the papers had been signed.

"I'm sure you will." The older man gripped my elbow and squeezed my hand, clearly intending to convey a dominance over me he didn't have.

He could knock himself out if it made him feel more secure. I knew how good I was. I didn't need to white-knuckle the old man to prove it. The deal would make the firm a lot of money, but there was nothing one-sided about it. With the potential pitfalls involved in navigating international markets and regulations, Gulf Enterprises was lucky to get us. At any price. I was feeling pretty damn satisfied. And then my phone buzzed with an incoming text.

I always turned my phone off during meetings but I'd been so caught up waiting for Alex to text, I'd forgotten.

"Do you need to get that?" asked the older man, arching a brow.

I glanced at our joined hands and realized my grip had involuntarily tightened at the sound of the incoming message.

"No, of course not," I said, relaxing my hand and reaching up to clap him reassuringly on the back a second before my pocket started to talk.

Fuck. I'd left the text-to-voice app open. Losing what was left of my cool, I reached inside my pocket to silence the phone but not before it broadcast its message to everyone within earshot.

"I came again. In the tub this time."

The computer-generated voice did nothing to hide the meaning of the message. If anything, it made the whole thing that much worse.

"Client?" asked the company's PR person, not bothering to hide his grin.

The owner didn't look amused, and I could see Jared in my peripheral vision looking like he'd be happy to take a bat to my Porsche. I couldn't blame him. I shut off the phone but the damage was done.

"No, sir. That was personal. I apologize."

The older man nodded but it was clear from his expression exactly what he thought about his attorneys having personal lives. At least we still were his attorneys. Despite my colossal lapse in judgment, I could still spin this as a win.

He made a noncommittal noise, and I said a silent prayer of gratitude that Alex's text came in after the papers had been signed. Of course, if I hadn't had my head up my ass and remembered to turn off the app, it wouldn't have mattered either way.

Jared circled around the table, submitting to his own round of Vulcan death grip handshakes before walking the team to the top of the stairs. I took the opportunity to slip the phone from my pocket and open Alex's message, without the sound this time. The picture was worse.

"Who do you have waiting for you in the tub?" asked Jared from too close behind me. "And here I thought your problem was blue balls-induced stress."

I stuffed the phone in my pocket, not caring that I looked guilty as hell. There was no way on God's green earth I was sharing Alex's photo with Jared.

"No one." He wouldn't buy it, but I had to try.

"Fuck you."

"Nice talk. We did it." I tapped the signed contract still sitting on the table, hoping to distract him.

"Yeah, yeah, we get to learn international shipping regulations. Woo-hoo. Who's in the tub?" He collapsed back in his seat and pinned me with his courtroom glare, the one he used with hostile witnesses. "Wait a minute. It's Dr. Smithson, isn't it? The Dom trainer. She's the reason you ditched the case." His eyes went so wide his eyebrows hit his hairline. "Dom whisperer is more like it if she's got you this fucked up."

I pressed my lips together. Unless I looked him in the eye and lied my ass off, he was going to find out about Alex.

"Holy shit!" he said, loud enough to make other diners glance in our direction.

"I don't think they heard you on the other side of the Quarter."

"Holy shit." He pitched his voice artificially low but his eyebrows were still trying to bury themselves in his hairline. "You are so screwed. Who else knows? The other partners?"

"No and they won't. Not unless you tell them."

I glared at him and he held his hand up in front of his face like the most unlikely Boy Scout on the face of the planet.

"I'm not telling. So what's the deal? You recuse yourself this morning and have her accounting for her orgasms by dinner? What the fuck, man?"

I didn't like how crazy it sounded when he laid it out like that. I directed things; I didn't react. Except with Alex. All bets were off where she was concerned.

"Remember the woman from the bar a couple of weeks ago?"

The speed with which he recalled the casual meeting was a testament to how long it had been since my friends saw me with a woman.

"The one with the redhead. I remember."

I waited for a moment while he puzzled through things.

"No way. She's Dr. Smithson? The one you were trying to ruin this morning?"

I nodded, letting the realization settle over him at the same time it all came rushing back to me.

"The Lexi responsible for the clusterfuck at the club? No shit." He blew out his breath and shook his head.

"That about sums it up."

"So what happened? You had a colossal hard-on for her this morning," he said, grinning at his choice of words. "I remember talk of 'burying the reckless woman who had no clue what she was playing at.' How did you get from there to here?"

"I got her to agree to take me through a session." I left out the paying her part. I was already on legal ground so shaky I could go under at any moment. I didn't need to add to the quicksand.

"I'm not sure whether to bow to your awesomeness or run before the lightning strikes. You're either a genius or totally fucked."

Or both, I thought.

"It didn't work out exactly the way I'd planned." *Understatement of the century.*

"I don't know, man. She's calling to tell you she got herself off in the tub. It seems to me that has promise."

He gave me a shit-eating grin and I felt my lips curving in spite of the warning alarms going off in my head.

"Maybe."

"Are you going to bring her to the club? It's been a long damn time since you played in public. What better way to teach her what she doesn't know?"

Jared had a point. I couldn't explain why the idea didn't sit well with me, but something about taking Alex to play at the club felt off. I was going to continue letting my gut run the show. For now at least.

"It's too soon." It was a bullshit answer but it was the best I could give him.

"For her or for you?" he asked, clearly skeptical.

"Both maybe."

"You've got to know, but don't wait too long. Julie's been gone a long time."

Hearing him say my ex's name caught me off guard and I realized she didn't even play into my decision not to take Alex to Bacchus. *Interesting.*

The server appeared with two rocks glasses of Scotch and the chef's apologies. Apparently Matt was too busy in the kitchen to join us. It had been a long shot. The restaurant was packed.

"No worries," said Jared, winking at the pretty young woman. "At least he sends exceptional presents."

She smiled at him and shook her head, clearly over him before he even got started. Smart woman. I took a swallow of the smoky amber liquid, wondering how long I was going to have to wait before I could ditch my nosey friend and figure out how I wanted to respond to Alex's text.

"Was there something else on your mind?" I tossed it out there all casual like but I could tell by the arch of his eyebrow he wasn't buying it.

"Why yes actually, there was. Unless you have somewhere else you need to be? Like maybe in a tub somewhere?"

"Shut up. What is it?"

"I'm just messing with you. It can wait until the morning. Sounds like you've got your hands full. Or are about to," he said, grinning. "I'm glad. You've been alone too long. And unlike me, one-night hookups never really seemed to do it for you."

I opened my mouth to tell him it wasn't like that— that I was still alone. Whatever Alex and I were doing, it wasn't a long-term relationship. But when I started to speak, I realized I didn't want to say the words out loud. *How fucked up was that?*

"Thanks." I should stay and talk until Jared was ready to go, but it felt like my phone with Alex's photo was burning a hole in my jacket pocket.

"Go on," he said, waving me away. "I'm going to head downstairs to the bar for a bit. See if I can find someone new to the city in need of some company."

I didn't wait. I shook his hand and headed for the exit. My phone was in my hand before I hit the bottom of the stairs.

10

Alex

"OOH, WHAT'S IN THE FANCY box?" I asked, glancing at the boutique store package resting on Charlotte's orderly desk.

After we left the deposition, I'd gotten a dozen or so increasingly demanding texts from her, culminating with an admonition to get my pretty little ass into her office at nine or she'd show me what a flogger could really do. She was tiny; I could take her. But I loved her so I hauled my butt into her office in the morning to answer questions I'd much rather avoid.

"I have many, many questions." She peered at me over the top of her reading glasses, managing to look like a cross between a sexy Alice in Wonderland and an angry nun. "But since you went first, you tell me. Why is Erik Jensen, Esq., sending gifts addressed to you from *Les Bains de Mer* to my office?"

"It's from him?" I asked, taking a step back and staring at the pale-blue box printed with delicate white shells as if it might hold a snake. *That's what did in Cleopatra, right?* Not that I was comparing myself to the Egyptian queen or anything, but trust a dangerous man and the next thing you knew, you were getting snake deliveries.

"Open it, and then start talking. Or better yet, talk while you open. What the actual fuck, Alex?"

"I don't know why he sent the box here." I hadn't given him my home address, but with the resources his offices had, I was sure he had it already. And if he hadn't wanted to send it there, I knew he had my post office box. It was on the contact on my website. That he'd sent the box to Charlotte meant one of two things: either he was trying to poke at me and wanted witnesses or, more alarming, he read me well enough already to know seeing my friend would be one of the first things I did in the morning. Bolstering my courage, I picked up the box and carried it to the small sofa, letting it rest on my lap while I worked up the nerve to open it. I didn't know the store but it wasn't likely to include sex toys or anything. And if it did, I could explain them away. It would be a lot more comfortable to have Charlotte think Erik was making fun of my profession than explain why he'd be sending me thoughtful gifts.

"Let's revisit the where," she said, sounding like her patience had started to fray. "And move on to the why."

"I don't know that either." Honestly, the only thing I had a real shot at was the *what*. Setting the lid of the box to the side, I peered inside. Nestled in the palest green-blue tissue paper was a collection of glass bottles filled with liquids the color of sea glass. The elegant handwritten labels with words like *Aphrodite's Pearl* and *Mermaid's Dreams* wrapped the slender bottles, and there was a huge natural sea sponge tucked into the side of the box, with a card resting on top. Ignoring Charlotte's impatient noises for a moment, I slid the pure white cardstock from the envelope.

THANK YOU FOR THE GIFT. USE THIS NEXT TIME AND IMAGINE IT'S MY HAND, OR TONGUE. YOUR CHOICE—THIS TIME.

I shoved the card back into the envelope and buried it under the tissue paper. Not that it was likely to deter my friend from finding out everything. My face was scorching hot, and I knew I must have blushed beet-red. I'd sent Erik the picture of me in the tub on impulse. Regardless of what I might think about whatever this thing was we were doing, I wanted to at least try. There was no reason to pretend and about a dozen great ones not to go through with any of it. If I was doing it, I was going to really do it. The one orgasm in the elevator hadn't done a thing to satisfy me, so I'd taken matters into my own hand again in the tub. Per our agreement, I sent him a text letting him know. The picture had been an afterthought. It only showed my calves and feet extending out of the sea of bubbles. I thought it might be a way to spread some of the torture around. Apparently, it inspired him.

"I'm going to rephrase my question and you're going to answer it. Where did you go after you left the deposition?"

I paused, knowing there was no way I could tell her what happened without her going ballistic.

"He cornered me in the lobby after the deposition and dared me to take him through a session." I said the words as quickly as I could, like ripping off a Band-Aid.

"You didn't." She shook her head in a way that made it clear she already knew the answer.

"I did," I said and braced for impact.

"Please tell me you didn't have sex with the man," Charlotte said, coming out from behind her desk to sit next to me.

"No. Of course not," I said, ignoring how much I'd wanted to and opting for righteous indignation instead.

"So what did you do?"

"We walked around a bit, had beignets and talked." I distilled the encounter down to as few words as I thought my friend might accept.

"You talked? Talked about what exactly?"

"Nothing much really. A little dominance and submission. That's about it."

"Did you talk about the case? Tell me the truth, Alex. It's important." She shifted to face me, and I saw the concern clear in her eyes.

She'd give me shit because it's what she did, but she loved me so she'd always look out for me. I reached for her hand and gave it a squeeze. I didn't want to tell anyone about what happened with Kyle. I'd been replaying the conversation in my head, catching myself thinking about the timid man wielding a cane. I didn't need Erik to tell me I bore some responsibility for what happened and it didn't sit well. I'd told him the truth when I said I wanted to help people. The money was nice—hell, great— but I'd felt like I was providing a service. Not exactly a naked Dr. Ruth but helpful.

"He told me why he took the case and why it was personal."

"And? God, it's like pulling teeth with you this morning."

"Does attorney-client privilege protect him too?" We hadn't talked about not sharing each other's secrets. The fact that we both had them made the conversation unnecessary. But the same wasn't true for Charlotte. I had to tell her something. She'd never let me out of her office if I didn't and when I thought logically about it, I wanted to talk to her about what I'd found out about Kyle. Get another perspective from someone who got paid to look at things objectively. But I didn't want to out Erik, and I didn't want anything he'd told me to come back and bite him in the ass.

"Privilege covers you, Alex. My job is to look out for you. Jensen can take care of himself."

"Promise me that what I tell you stays between us. You won't use it."

I could tell by the thin crease in her forehead and the set of her mouth that she didn't like it, but she nodded.

"Erik is a member at a BDSM club."

She arched an eyebrow at me. I was pretty sure it was over my use of his first name and not the BDSM bit.

"A client of mine was a patron at the club. Things got out of hand and the dungeon monitor had to step in." I swear, even after all these years, I couldn't think those words without replacing monitor with master and remembering the tiny *Lord of the Rings* figures I'd had in junior high. "He'd caned a woman to the point where he broke her skin. When they were throwing him out, he said he knew what he was doing because Lexi taught him." I let the words hang in the space between us. I wasn't about to try to sugarcoat them or pretend what happened was less horrific than it actually was.

"Jesus." Charlotte blew the word out on a breath and then jumped up and headed to her desk. "You're going to need a new attorney."

"What? No."

"Alex, if this dungeon or anybody else involved in this tries to sue you, the liability could be huge. Listen, I know you. I get that you feel responsible, but this isn't something to fuck around with. I don't think there's grounds for criminal charges, but you need somebody who knows about this kind of liability to handle it," she said, reaching for the phone on her desk.

"There's nothing to handle." A new kind of fear settled in the pit of my stomach. I didn't think the antacids would make a dent in this kind of anxiety. "The dungeon isn't going to sue. They'd be opening themselves up to some kind of liability too, right? Not to mention the extra scrutiny, which I can't imagine they'd want." I thought back over what Erik had told me about the submissive. "I don't think the woman will sue either. Erik—Jensen said she egged my client on. She's into that kind of pain." I fought back the shudder. I wasn't about to judge someone for whatever turned them on, but I'd always had a hard time understanding extreme masochists. Walking the pleasure/pain line—sure—but cutting, needles, pain that left permanent marks? That I didn't understand.

"And your client?"

"No way. He was crazy private. There's no way he'd call that kind of attention to himself. He'd never initiate it anyway."

Charlotte looked skeptical but she let go of the receiver and dropped into her chair.

"I don't like it."

"I don't love it myself." That was the understatement of the century.

I moved the box from my lap to the empty seat beside me and smoothed my sweaty palms over my skirt. Charlotte's gaze shifted to Erik's gift the way I imagined a hawk tracked a rabbit's movements.

"What does Jensen want with you?"

Lots of things I was pretty sure I didn't want to explain to my friend, no matter how close we were. I went for the easiest one.

"He says he's a Dom. I think he wants to teach me stuff."

"I don't even know where to start with that. Naked stuff? I thought you worked with a guy before you started seeing private clients."

I thought back to the Dom I'd met with before I opened the Gentleman's Submissive. Whatever he may have been, he and Erik weren't in the same league. I'd felt more fully clothed with Erik than I'd ever felt with Master Whatshisname. I was starting to realize some of that might have had more to do with my attitude and willingness to let go of control than the men involved. I remembered Erik's voice in my ear when I'd been blindfolded. His hand warm and strong through his jacket against the small of my back.

Some of it was the man.

"I did, but that doesn't mean I can't learn more. I won't say it out loud, to anyone but you, but I do feel responsible for what happened with my client. I don't want to let something like that ever happen again."

She smoothed a hand over her already perfectly smooth chignon, and I got a rare glimpse at her internal struggle. Charlotte made a living hiding her thoughts and feelings and only showing people what she wanted them to see. We had that in common.

"So what kind of things did you and Jensen do? Naked things?" Her lips curved in the barest smirk, and the band around my chest relaxed a fraction. If she could tease me, I could believe things were going to be okay.

"He put my clothes on," I said, remembering the way the backs of his fingers brushed my breasts as he'd fastened the buttons on my blouse, the silk adding its own kind of sensuality to his touch.

"You stripped for him?"

"Naked is my best battle armor, and the lack of blood flow to the brain usually works in my favor."

"But it didn't with Jensen?" she asked, smiling for real this time.

"Nope. It did not."

"Are you going to see him again?"

"He already paid for a second session," I said, thinking of the ease with which he'd dropped another grand into my bank account and the pressure it relieved. Financial pressure anyway. His *don't come without telling me* thing added its own kind of pressure.

It seemed like a lot of money, and it was, but with the rent on my studio, my personal living expenses, and no money coming in, I was going to have to stretch to make it work.

"Is it okay for me to see other clients?"

Charlotte shook her head and my spirits dipped a notch. "Jensen is defying his own order by paying you. Although he's on shaky enough ground for the stunt he pulled during the deposition. I doubt he'd breathe a word about it. The cease-and-desist is still in place. For now," she added when I blew out a breath. "I put a call into Jensen's firm to see who would be taking over for him. I haven't heard back yet." She paused for a minute, thinking. "If whoever takes over doesn't have such a hard-on for you"—she smirked at the pun, and I managed to smile back—"maybe I can get them to settle the whole thing. The push to go to trial didn't make any sense before, but if it was Jensen and not the client pushing, we should be able to make it go away quickly."

I felt my smile widen. Whatever else might be going on, getting out from under the lawsuit would be a relief.

Alex

I DID YOGA, MOSTLY BECAUSE in order to eat everything I liked and not weigh three hundred pounds, I had to do something. I walked a lot. Living in a city like New Orleans necessitated it, but if I wanted to indulge in pralines and Erik's beignets, I needed to do more. Stretching, even adventure stretching like Meredith and I did at the yoga studio downtown a couple of times a week, was nothing compared to the kind of hell the personal trainer seemed intent on putting me through.

Apparently a session with the trainer was part of the new member welcome package. The gift membership a client gave me was set to expire in a couple of months. Despite owning a string of gyms and having the body to show for it, the man had been surprisingly reticent. I helped him boost his confidence and the last I'd heard, he and his new wife were expecting their first child. And I no longer had the excuse of being too busy with work to put off going.

"Push, push, push," said the twenty-something drill sergeant in perfectly pressed flat-front chino shorts and a white polo with the club's logo embroidered over what I bet was an impressive pec. The stupid uniform made it impossible to know for sure, which was wrong on so many levels. If I was going to do something that made me sweat so much and hurt so bad, I ought to at least have something nice to look at. Motivation and shit.

I pushed against the bar over my head, giving it everything I had, and watched it move all of two inches before I let go and it slid back to its starting position.

"That's okay," he said, more like he was trying to reassure himself than me that I'd eventually get it. "We'll lower the weight and up the reps. In a couple of weeks, you'll be hitting the top."

I couldn't think about doing this for a couple of weeks. I'd rather be flogged by a firm full of accountants than spend that much time in the gym trying to make weights move for no good reason. I let Commander Ken lead me through a series of leg exercises. They were easier for me than arms and by the time we finished, some of his will to live seemed to have come back even as mine had seeped away. I made it through a minute of plank and called uncle when we hit V sits.

"That was fantastic," I said, trying and failing to hide the fact that I was gasping for breath. "Just great. Thanks for showing me around." I struggled to my feet, ignoring my trembling legs so I could escape while I had the chance. I stuck out my hand to shake and after a moment, he took it.

I could tell by the confused expression on his face, he hadn't been ready to finish. I kept my smile glued in place and he had no choice but to push for more or shake my hand. I watched him wrestle with the options before finally deciding to take my hand.

"Great job today," he said with an amazing amount of generosity.

I arched an eyebrow at him and his can-do façade slipped for a moment. He gave me a genuine smile. I might have worked harder if he'd shown me that instead of the *rah-rah, push harder* cheerleader stuff we'd been doing for the past forty-five minutes. I thought about telling him, but it probably wouldn't have made a difference and it seemed better to let both of us off the hook as soon as possible.

I needed a shower, but after all that time heaving weights around, I needed sustenance more. I'd remember seeing something about an apres workout café. I doubted they'd have anything as fortifying as a decent donut, but made right, a smoothie could be almost as good as a milkshake. Not the chocolate or salted caramel kind but better than wheatgrass. Making my way past the workout-driven minions to the mezzanine level, I placed my order for a berry smoothie, ignoring the look the girl behind the counter gave me when I asked if it could be made with whole milk yogurt and honey instead of agave.

Given her expression when she handed me the glass, I might as well have been asking her to smear butter on my thighs. With all the straining I'd done, I had to at least have worked off some yogurt. If not, I didn't want to know. Ignorance is bliss and all.

I found a seat at the bar looking out over the machines below, and sucked a swallow of my full-fat berry extravaganza through the wider-than-normal straw. At least they didn't make it hard to get to the good stuff. I could maybe even get used to this. I could sit on my barstool, sucking on smoothies for a couple of weeks and call it using my gym membership. Of course, that would be going in the wrong direction where the size of my ass was concerned.

Ignoring the way my abs ached as I leaned forward, I scanned the crowd below. *If only people watching burned calories.* There was a guy—broad shoulders, great ass—pounding the treadmill like he was running away from something. At this distance, it was hard to tell but it looked like he was wearing earbuds. I wondered what kind of music he listened to that made him run like that. *Erik could probably run like that. He had the body for it.* I mean, I hadn't seen all of it, but I'd felt a lot of it and I had high hopes for the rest. He wouldn't run in a place like this. Regardless of how high-end it might be, it was still too public for a man like Erik. He probably had a treadmill in his loft, where he could run looking out over the Gulf.

My mind drifted from Erik running to Erik naked in the shower, washing the sweat off his completely lickable body. Taking his heavy cock in his hand and running a soapy fist down the length. I inadvertently sucked harder on the straw and coughed when I choked on the berry smoothie. I should have tried to find a way to make our *text me before you come* arrangement reciprocal. Even as I had the thought, I heard Jack Nicholson ala *A Few Good Men,* saying "You can't handle the texts." Nicholson was right. I probably couldn't handle knowing when Erik was getting off. *What if it was with someone else?*

The thought did uncomfortable things to a place deep inside my chest. And then it twisted itself around and a little slice of genius was born. I slipped my phone out of the nifty Lycra sleeve I'd gotten to hold it while I pumped iron and scrolled to the contact for Sir.

YOU DON'T NEED ME TO TEXT YOU IF I'M HAVING AN ORGASM WITH SOMEONE ELSE, RIGHT? THAT WOULD JUST BE WEIRD.

The reply came so fast; he must have been staring at the phone when he got the text.

DON'T DO IT

It would be easy to let him off the hook, but honestly, where was the fun in that?

K. I WON'T TELL YOU

NOT WAT I MEANT AND YOU NO IT

If the typos were any indication, I'd succeeded in getting under his skin at least a little.

YOU'RE A LAWYER. YOU OUGHT TO BE BETTER AT COMMUNICATING.

The pause before my phone vibrated was so long I'd almost convinced myself he'd given up.

I DO NOT WANT YOU TO HAVE ORGASMS WITH ANYONE ELSE.

NOT OPEN FOR NEGOTIATION. HARD LIMIT.

His commander-in-chief tone would have pissed me off if I wasn't so sure I'd riled him. That was still no reason to let him get away with it.

I DON'T WANT TO SPEND THE REST OF THE DAY CLEANING MY APARTMENT. DUST BUNNIES DON'T CARE ABOUT THE LIMITS HARD OR OTHERWISE. SAYING A THING DOESN'T MAKE IT SO.

DON'T TEST ME, KITTEN

Again with the kitten thing. Yeesh, I ought to accuse him of being some kind of crazy cat man. I was working out how to phrase it for the maximum amount of burn (and actively ignoring the way my pulse kicked up whenever he said it because I wasn't anybody's pet) when I shifted on my seat and almost fell off the stool. I overcorrected and had to grip the counter to stop from landing on my ass and put a sizeable dent in my smoothie cup. Taking it as a sign not to poke the sleeping tiger, rile Nicholson, or tempt karma in any other way where Jensen was concerned, I ditched the cup and shoved my phone back in the handy pouch without responding.

I got out of the club as fast as my abused legs could carry me. The last thing I needed was an overzealous personal trainer catching me on the way out to try to schedule more weight-induced torture. I needed food you had to chew. Smoothies were beverages, not meals, and I hadn't been lying to Erik when I said I had to clean my apartment. I wasn't obsessive about it, at least not in a clinical way, but I needed to keep my spaces orderly. My life worked better that way.

I lived in an older building just outside the district, a couple of blocks from my studio. With its cast-iron railings and long plantation shutters, I'd fallen in love with the place the first time I saw it. It was so unlike where I'd grown up and practically oozed Creole charm. It was also dusty, a little cramped, and it went from charming to hovel fast if I didn't stay on top of it. I'd been so preoccupied with the threat of the lawsuit and work worries, it had been too long since I'd given it a good cleaning. I could probably write notes to myself in the layer of dust on the old dresser I used as a hall table.

Technically the gym was in walking distance of my place. Walking was the one exercise I didn't normally shun but given the way my legs felt after all the lifts the polo-clad drill sergeant made me do, I figured I'd be dragging myself the last few blocks to my apartment if I tried to walk, so I splurged on an Uber. Erik hadn't sent another text, and I spent way too much time rationalizing in my head the fact that there was nothing for him to respond to since I hadn't replied to his last one and I didn't care anyway. Lies, all of it, but there was a reason denial was a thing.

Sometimes the best way to preserve mental health was to avoid looking too closely at things. Okay, that was a total crock of shit and I knew it but it didn't stop me from using it to quiet the *what's Erik thinking/who's he doing* whirlwind blowing through my head. I hated it when women spent all their time thinking about men. The last thing I wanted to do was become one of them. *I* owned my power, not some guy with an exceptional ass and the kind of mind that took sparring to a new, sexier level.

I made a quick stop at the bakery on Bienville. They didn't have a storefront. The bulk of their business was supplying bread for po 'boys to local restaurants, but if you knew which door to bang on, they'd sell a loaf or two if they had leftovers. Leftover bread from the bakery was better than any bread I'd ever had before I moved to New Orleans. Crusty on the outside and lighter than air on the inside. My mouth started to water, thinking about it. I didn't have to knock on the ancient painted wood door. It was open when I got there. I handed the older man standing in the shadow of the doorway a couple of dollars and he handed me a paper-wrapped loaf like some kind of clandestine yeasty drug trade.

Clutching my score to my chest so I wouldn't be tempted to rip it open and shove chunks of the crusty deliciousness into my mouth while I was still out on the street, I hobbled the last half a block to my apartment. I climbed the narrow wooden stairs to the second floor, certain my legs would give out any minute and I'd be left sprawled in the stairwell with nothing to sustain me but a loaf of bread until one of my neighbors took pity on me and called for help.

I heard bumping and what sounded like furniture being dragged over the floor above. Mr. Roulaine lived in the only other apartment on my floor. He was every bit of seventy, and I hated the idea of him trying to move furniture by himself. The idea of the sweet old man dropping from a heart attack gave me a second wind, and I managed to hoist myself the last few steps to the top of the stairs. I glanced from his closed door to mine and back again.

The noise was coming from my apartment, which didn't make any sense at all. I stood in the hallway close enough to the top of the steps to make a run for it—controlled fall would be more like it—if I needed to, and tried to figure out what to do. I'd never been one of those women who hear a noise in the creepy basement and go investigate. I was more of the *wait outside on the porch for the cops to come* kind of woman, but calling the police in this case felt like overkill. I clutched my bread, debating my next move when my apartment door opened, and a pleasant-looking woman emerged, carrying the biggest vacuum cleaner I'd ever seen. It looked like a jet engine with a handle and bag attached.

"Oh hello," she said, pausing in her attempt to wrestle the vacuum to the top of the narrow flight of steps. "You must be Ms. Smithson. We'll be finished up and out of your hair in just a minute."

"I'm sorry. Who are you? Finished with what?" Maybe the post-workout endorphins were messing with me and I'd forgotten I'd invited a group of people to my apartment, but I didn't think so.

"Mr. Jensen hired us to clean your apartment. I hope I didn't ruin the surprise. I assumed you knew."

Her pretty face looked stricken, and I relaxed my forehead and pasted what I hoped was a friendly smile on my face. It wasn't her fault Erik Jensen was an assuming know-it-all bastard who'd gotten someone to break into my apartment. And if the vacuum and the Happy Housekeepers logo on her navy polo was any indication, she and her crew had taken cleaning off my to-do list for the day.

"It's okay. Thank you," I added, hoping I was right about the cleaning thing and that they weren't part of some kind of elaborate petty burglary ring.

She flashed me a quick grateful smile as she resumed dragging the massive vacuum down the steps. I took a few tentative steps toward my front door, uncertain what I was supposed to do since there were still people inside. Calling Jensen and telling him to stay the fuck out of my apartment was at the top of my list, but I wasn't sure I wanted an audience for that. Before I could decide, the door opened and people all wearing navy polos and carrying a variety of cleaning paraphernalia filed past me. It was like watching a clown car empty out of my small apartment.

"All finished," said the last one through.

The young woman held the door open for me, and I murmured my thanks as I entered my cleaned to within an inch of its life space. There wasn't a speck of dust or a smudge anywhere and the place smelled like a delicious combination of lemon and lavender. I set the bread on my spotless kitchen table and crossed the immaculate living room with its freshly vacuumed carpet—it was almost a different shade of aubergine. I didn't want to think about how much dirt the Happy Housekeeper people must have gotten out of it. I pushed open the bathroom door and decided I'd sell a kidney if I had to to get them to come back every month.

My towels were stacked in perfect order and the cosmetics I'd left in disarray on the counter had been organized and tucked neatly into their spots. The pale-blue box holding the bath oils Erik sent me sat on top of a fluffy folded white towel. It was like walking into my own personal spa. I stood frozen in the doorway, trying to choose between soaking my abused muscles in my scrupulously clean tub, eating my fresh bread, or calling Erik and—I couldn't decide between thanking him or yelling at him. It was hard to stay angry when faced with so many delicious choices and an unscheduled afternoon stretching out in front of me. That didn't mean I wouldn't try.

My phone buzzing with an incoming text managed to unstick my feet. I slid open the screen and saw a new message from Sir. *Yep, I could definitely try.*

PROBLEM SOLVED. NOW YOU DO WHAT I WANT.

My finger hovered over the screen, responses already flooding my head. The words were coming too fast for a text so I hit the Call icon and waited for Erik to answer. I didn't have to wait long. There was only one ring before I heard his voice, warm and rich with just enough of a drawl to feel like melted caramel washing over me, on the other end of the line.

"Yes, kitten."

Any indecisiveness I'd been feeling vanished at his greeting.

"I'm not your fucking pet."

"Not yet, but you will be. My *fucking* pet." He laced the word with enough heat to let me know exactly what he was thinking.

I used sex as power often enough to know exactly what he was doing, but there was something else there too. Something that made me believe he'd enjoy every minute of it. The sex more than the power. It was the opposite of the way I usually felt about it. I hated it but my body responded, and I pressed my legs together to ease the ache I didn't want to feel.

"You had no business breaking into my apartment." In my mind, I had a thousand comebacks, most of which started with *you arrogant fucking prick*, but breaking and entering was the first complete thought I could get hold of.

"*I* didn't break into your apartment. I had someone let the cleaning crew in to take care of the dust bunnies so we could concentrate on the hard limits."

I wanted to hate the ease he used to throw my words back at me, but I couldn't help but admire him a bit too. The man was arrogant and assuming to a fault, but he got shit done. Competence was the new sexy where I was concerned.

"Now you have the afternoon to take a bath," he said as if him saying it made it so.

It pissed me off that his suggestion mirrored what I'd been planning to do.

"When you slide your fingers inside your sweet pussy, I want you to imagine it's my hand touching you. My hand bringing you to the edge of orgasm over and over before finally making you come. My fingers your hot cunt clenches around when you can't hold back any longer." He dropped his voice as he spoke until it was a low rumble in my ear, linking his words to my throbbing clit.

I hated that he could make me feel so much without even touching me—hell, without even being in the same room. But I was curious too, both about my response to him and how much more he could make me feel. I had no trouble getting myself off, but in my experience, sex with a partner was adequate at best. I didn't need to do it to know that sex with Erik would be anything but adequate. I didn't need to do it but I wanted to. Not that I would. Unless I did. *Fuck.*

"We can consider this your notification that you're going to come. Although, I'd love another picture or two of you in the tub. Have you had a chance to try what I sent you?"

My brain stuttered for a moment, trying to catch up with his words and then I realized something.

"Why did you send the bath stuff to Charlotte's office when you knew my home address?" I'd assumed he didn't have it or hadn't bothered to look it up. But if he'd done it just to embarrass me in front of my friend, I wanted to know.

"I didn't want to cross that boundary until you invited me to."

"So what's changed? I sure as hell didn't invite you to my apartment."

"I moved the boundary."

Of course he did.

"Take a bath, Alexandra. I want to book our next session for tomorrow. I'll pick you up at two."

I wanted to tell him I had plans, but with the cease-and-desist in place, we both knew I probably didn't. I wanted to tell him to go fuck himself, but a part of me I didn't like all that much wanted to tell him to fuck *me*. I settled for an eye roll he couldn't see and then hung up before I said something I'd regret.

ERIK

I OPENED THE PHOTO FOR about the hundredth time and stared at the image on the screen. I'd looked at it so many times I ought to make it my fucking wallpaper, but I couldn't stand the idea of anyone else seeing Alex like that, which was insane given her profession and the ease with which she shed her clothes. Feeling possessive was a new thing for me and one I wasn't entirely comfortable with.

The woman knew how to set a scene. An almost empty wineglass perched on the edge of the tub, its scarlet liquid a sharp contrast to the white porcelain. Her long legs stretched out in front of her, unobscured by bubbles. I'd sent her bath oil instead of bubble bath for exactly that reason. Rather than pretending to be shy, she'd taken full advantage of the water's translucency. I could clearly see the soft mound of her stomach and the gentle swell of her breasts. She'd cropped the picture just below her nipples but it was enough to remind me what it felt like to have her pebbled flesh, tight and aching against my palm with nothing more than the thin silk of her blouse between us. Or my new favorite thing to imagine: her skin with nothing but the slick of water and scented oil as a barrier.

It was her hand that captured my attention and made it hard for me to think of anything but replacing it with my own—a fact I was sure she was acutely aware of. Her palm covered her sex, her slender fingers sliding between her legs in a way that made my fucking mouth water. She'd sent the photos as I was getting ready to walk into a dinner meeting with a potential client I'd been courting for months and instead of giving the client my full attention, I found myself glancing at my phone, waiting for her hand to magically move and show me what I wanted to see. What I wanted to taste. It was like the best retro porn. Pure unadulterated sex without actually revealing anything, so I was left wanting so much more. I had no doubt she knew exactly what she was doing and my preoccupied—hell, fucking obsessed—state was her desired effect.

I'd stolen glances between courses and hoped that the client read my distraction as confidence and a lack of eagerness. We weren't the only firm trying to hook them. If I was lucky, the others had been so busy fawning over them, they'd find my apparent disinterest intriguing. Or more likely, it would be one more thing for the other partners to take me to task about. After the recusal debacle, I couldn't afford many more. I might be the boss, but I wasn't the only one and Jared knew me well enough to tell when I was bullshitting him. Coupled with the line I'd fed him the other night at dinner, it was only a matter of time before he put things together and realized I was fucked in the head over a woman.

None of that had stopped me from making plans for our session or from keeping those plans. It *would* stop me from having sex with Alex—for today at least, which was frustrating as hell. I couldn't remember a time I'd wanted a woman more. It was as if every single thing she did was designed to amplify that desire, which was exactly why we wouldn't be having sex. Regardless of how much I wanted to be inside her, we weren't doing it until I was sure she was willingly submitting and not just playacting.

I wanted the real thing or nothing at all. That was a lie. I wanted Alex any fucking way I could get her but I still had at least enough control to set and hold some standards for myself. I didn't want to be one more man she sharpened her blade against.

The town car pulled up in front of her building five minutes before I was scheduled to be there. I glanced up in time to see the curtain on her apartment window flutter closed. *So much for surprising her.* I opened the door, letting in a rush of low country heat and humidity so thick, it felt like I could cut it with a knife. It was hotter than normal for this time of year and felt like a storm building. An afternoon thunderstorm might break the tension and suit my purposes perfectly.

I strode to the entrance of her building, frowning when I found the door unlocked. It was one thing not to have a doorman. Most of the older buildings downtown didn't, but it was another thing entirely to leave the building open to any drunken tourist or homeless local to wander into the dark stairway and wait for the residents. That was unacceptable. I ignored the fact it had served my purpose with the cleaning crew. The ease with which I'd gained access to her apartment was one more thing to add to the list.

Ignoring it until I could figure out how to fix it, I hurried up the narrow stairs to the second floor. I scanned the doors, stopping in front of the one with the 2A stamped onto the cast-iron knocker. I raised my hand to rap on the door but it opened before I had a chance, revealing Alexandra dressed in the pale-pink pencil skirt and matching bra and sheer blouse I'd had my personal shopper deliver. The nude-colored pumps were hers and if she'd followed my directions, they were the only other things she was wearing. I couldn't wait to find out if she'd obeyed me.

Her expression was a mixture of irritated and interested, and for the moment at least, it looked like interested was winning. Sending her clothes had been a stroke of genius. She was so used to taking her clothes off; I was determined to keep putting them back on her. And if I left off a piece or two, it only emphasized her vulnerability, something I was pretty sure she didn't feel when she was totally naked.

"Good afternoon, kitten." Honestly, pet names didn't really do it for me, but I loved seeing the way her eyes flashed when I said the word.

"What's up, pup?"

Laughter erupted from my throat, ending with a very undignified snort. *This woman—this sexy smart-ass—was going to be the death of me.*

"Point taken, Alexandra," I said, crowding her until she gave in and took a step back against the wall.

I didn't want to physically intimidate her—not exactly—but I needed to be the one who set the tone, and I couldn't afford to let her start to top from the bottom or we'd never get to the place I wanted to be. The kind of dominance and submission power play that could turn the exchange into a duet, into music we made together and not just two people performing side by side.

I leaned in until I felt the breath from her parted lips on my face. Her eyes were wide, pupils dilated and I'd bet much more than the thousand dollars I'd paid her for the session that she was wet and ready for me. Ready to find out how fucking perfectly we fit together. I hated it for both of us that we needed to wait. It would be so much easier to close the fraction of an inch between us and kiss her until we ended up back inside her apartment, and I ended up inside her. Easier but so much less satisfying. At least that was the lie I told myself as I stepped away from her without giving in to the urge to taste.

"Ready?" I asked, pressing my hand to the small of her back and guiding her in front of me.

"Always," she said, confidently striding forward away from my touch and leaving me no choice but to follow her.

NO PANTIES. ERIK sent me clothing. In my size, of course, and if I was feeling charitable, I'd have to admit what he'd chosen fit my taste. I wasn't feeling charitable because he'd also commanded I show up for our date wearing nothing but the clothes he'd chosen and the shoes I'd worn to the deposition. No hose, no panties. Nothing else.

It made me crazy. I'd shaved—I usually did as part of my work uniform—but for some reason, I felt more naked than if I'd been wearing a G-string. I think it was the contrast between the demure pencil skirt that hit below my knee and the smooth skin between my legs. It was like I had some kind of naughty secret and it made me way too aware, almost to the point of obsession of my bare sex. I'd been wet since I slipped into the expensive lace bra and sheer blouse that practically screamed classy sex, and so distracted I hadn't been able to sit down while I waited for Erik. I'd hovered around the window, watching for his car, only bringing myself to move when he finally pulled up.

The pup crack had been a spur-of-the-moment thing, but when he called me kitten again, I had to do something. I hated to admit it, but he knew some things about dominance and submission that I didn't. I was willing—hell, eager even—to learn more, but the pet thing had to go. Calling me kitten seemed like a step down a road I wasn't willing to travel. I was never going to wear a collar or a leash for anyone.

That didn't mean there weren't a lot of things I was willing to do with Erik. Starting with kissing and ending up hopefully with him as naked as I felt.

Except he didn't kiss me. He backed me up against the wall so I had no choice but to breathe in the spicy scent of his aftershave and feel the heat coming off his body in waves. He held his lips a fraction of an inch away from mine until I thought I might lose my mind with wanting the bastard. And then he moved away without closing the deal. He planted his hand on my back and tried to steer me like we were some kind of old married couple on our way to dinner at the country club.

That was a lie. There wasn't a single old married people thing about the way his palm burned through the thin silk of the blouse he'd chosen for me. Combined with the overwhelming awareness of my bare sex and the residual ache of the kiss that never happened, it was too much. I hurried down the steps and away from his touch, grateful when the driver opened the door to the car parked at my curb.

The feeling evaporated the second he slid in beside me, taking up too much room in the expansive backseat. Seriously, it was like the Tardis—bigger on the inside, and it didn't matter a bit, there was still too much Erik everywhere I looked, from the amber Scotch waiting next to a pair of cut crystal rocks glasses to the scent of rich leather advertising money and power. And that didn't count the man sitting next to me, his muscular thigh brushing against mine, reminding me of what I didn't have on under my skirt.

I watched him from my side of the seat, waiting to see what new kind of mindfuckery he'd pull next. It was a

161

little like being trapped in an enclosed space with a tiger who may or may not be hungry. I couldn't read him. I didn't have any trouble messing with him, ignoring for the moment the fact that it often backfired. But I couldn't get a read on what he was thinking and he rarely reacted the way I expected. I felt head blind, and I didn't like it. Or maybe I did. I wasn't sure about anything anymore.

"What's on the menu today? No blindfolds? What are we doing? Handcuffs? Floggers? Assorted pastry?" I said, determined to keep poking until I got some kind of reaction I could work with.

"You'll see when we get there." He relaxed into the seat, appearing completely comfortable in his domain.

He wasn't squirming because his thighs were slick and he couldn't figure out what he wanted to do about it. There wasn't a single thing about his posture that hinted at the kind of conflict I felt.

"Tell me about your day, Alexandra."

"Why don't you tell me about yours? I'm not allowed to work, remember?" Needling him about the cease-and-desist wasn't nearly as satisfying as I thought it would be.

"I assumed you were more than just your work."

Well, hell, I'd walked into that one.

"You had my apartment cleaned and saw last night's bath. I figured that got you up to speed."

"Your bath may have derailed a deal I've been working on for months. I was walking into dinner with a potential client when I got your photo."

I resisted the urge to sorry/not sorry him. Admitting my picture had an effect on him was a rare kind of candor for him. I didn't want to wreck it.

"I spent the evening imagining it was my fingers inside you instead of yours. My cock was so hard for you I couldn't concentrate on anything else."

His words made me shift in my seat, my arousal already slick on my thighs. Knowing a picture of me had that kind of effect on a man like Erik was heady stuff. I glanced up and caught him watching, his piercing, dark gaze pinned on me in a way that made it clear he knew exactly what I was thinking. He grinned like a big cat who had his prey clearly in his sights, and he was just waiting for me to make a move before he pounced.

"You asked for the photo," I said, hoping I pulled off the *careful what you wish for* attitude and knowing before his grin widened, I'd failed.

"Yes, I did."

The car had taken us across the city to I-10. Asking him where we were going was useless, but that didn't mean I was helpless. I still had weapons at my disposal, and if I played it right, I might be able to do something about the ache between my thighs. Bare minimum, I could stop feeling so out of control.

"I'm trying to do everything you tell me to," I said with as much innocence as I could muster.

He snorted in disbelief the second the words were out of my mouth and then swallowed the sound when my leg landed on his lap. I'd hiked up my skirt and spread my legs, baring myself to him. The cool air on my exposed sex made me feel even more naked and for a moment, I was unsure of myself. Like I might have poked a sleeping bear or something. In my experience, this was the point where most men lost the ability to think clearly. Erik already said my photo had that effect on him, and I could feel the long, hard length of his cock against my bare calf, but he wasn't making any move to touch me and aside from his initial attempt to swallow his laughter, he seemed determined not to respond.

An image of Winston Churchill and that "going through hell" quote popped into my head and I had to fight to keep from slamming my legs closed. If I did that, all I'd have accomplished was embarrassing myself. Failure was not an option. Tipping my hips forward, I slid my foot up until the point of my heel dug into Erik's thigh. Not hard enough to hurt him—I didn't think he was into that—just hard enough to demand his attention. He lifted my foot, slid off my shoe and rested the sole of my foot against his thigh with nothing more than a friendly pat. *Fuck.*

"I'm not going to touch you, Alexandra," he said with the same tone I imagined he used with his secretary or the barista who made his morning coffee. There was no heat or admonition, nothing but a statement of fact.

"I thought you weren't into orgasm denial," I said, feeling like the sand was shifted out from underneath me. I slid my bare foot closer to the outline of his cock, clearly visible through the charcoal-gray fabric of his dress slacks. *The man had spectacular taste in clothes.*

"You're welcome to make yourself come if you need to. We can certainly count this as you letting me know." He waved a hand toward me, and I felt the air move over my exposed sex. "I'm just not going to participate."

In that moment, I hated him a little bit. I might have hated him a lot if it hadn't been my idea to show him all my stuff, and if I hadn't felt his cock twitch against my toes and seen the way his jaw tightened, as if he were trying hard to stay still. *He wanted me.* He didn't have to say it for me to be sure, and if he was having this much trouble with the idea of me masturbating in front of him, the reality was bound to be about a thousand times better. At least I hoped so.

At this point, my choice was to definitely wallow in embarrassment and self-pity now or maybe feel it later. The maybe came with a maybe not and in this case, I was willing to take the chance. *Plus orgasms.*

"If you're sure," I said, keeping my gaze locked on his jaw as I slid my fingers over my aching clit.

ERIK

I WAS GOING TO BREAK my teeth if I clenched my jaw any tighter. Every time I thought I had a handle on things, Alex managed to turn them upside down on me. I was sure my apparent disinterest would be enough to stop her. Although, in retrospect, I had no idea why I'd come to that conclusion. The woman hadn't backed away from a single challenge I issued. I should have known she'd double down on masturbating in front of me.

I couldn't pretend I didn't want her. My cock was so hard it ached in a way it hadn't since the blue ball days of my adolescence. She'd call me on my bullshit if I tried to deny it. That didn't mean I'd cave. If anything, it made my resolve stronger. There was no way in hell I'd touch her now. Not when she was back to using her sexuality as a weapon against me. Which left me two obvious choices. I could use every skill I'd gained in the courtroom to hide my emotions or I could give in to what I felt and get myself off next to her. Unzip my fly, take my cock in my hand and stroke from balls to head until I came with her.

Aside from the obvious appeal of orgasming and not having to fight the ongoing distraction for the next couple of hours, there was the additional benefit of throwing Alexandra further off her game. She was good—very good—at the sex-for-power thing but I didn't think even she could hide her body's reaction to me stroking one out in front of her. It would be mutual pleasure.

That thought decided it for me. I didn't want side-by-side pleasure. I wanted us to create something together, something bigger, more powerful than anything we could do on our own. Regardless of how hard—no fucking pun intended—it would make the next couple of hours for me. Reluctantly surrendering to delayed gratification, I shifted in the leather seat so I could turn to face her.

Cupping her foot gently, I moved it away from my cock, but instead of setting it to the side, I held it, not caressing it but simply resting one palm on her arch and the other on the top of her foot. Caging her. My gaze deliberately moved up her leg to the juncture of her thighs and her fingers, slick with her arousal, playing over her clit. She slipped a slender finger through her bare folds and rocked her hips as her pale-pink fingertip pressed into her opening.

It was mesmerizing. I could watch for hours, learning her rhythms, learning the way she liked to touch herself, pleasure herself. But I knew without seeing her face this was a performance and the way she touched herself had more to do with manipulating me than it did with pleasing herself. I wouldn't learn anything I wanted to know from that.

My gaze trailed up her body over the gentle swell of her breasts covered in lace and the sheerest silk. The hard points of her nipples were clearly visible through the fabric, and I could tell she was genuinely aroused. But when my gaze found her face, I also knew I'd been right about her performing. Instead of eyes hooded with desire and a face flushed with passion, her expression was shrewd. Calculating. I pinned her with my gaze, commanding her attention, and waited.

Her shoulders stilled, and I knew without looking that she'd stopped stroking her clit. As I watched, her expression shifted from confusion to frustration. It was as if without an audience, she didn't know what to do. Like she'd be okay with me watching her fuck her pussy with her hand, but looking in her eyes when she came was somehow too intimate. It was perfect.

"We'll arrive in a few minutes, Alexandra. If you still want to come." I threw the words out as if it didn't matter one way or another, but I kept my gaze hooked on hers. This was where it could go wrong. If she decided to deny herself rather than give me an authentic glimpse at her pleasure, then this whole thing would be nothing more than a useless power struggle between us that cemented us each more firmly in our own camps instead of drawing us closer together. "I know I want you to," I said, offering her something genuine and hoping she'd reciprocate.

Her expression shifted again—the woman was a gorgeous chameleon, wearing her emotions on her face— and there was uncertainty in her dark eyes.

"For me, please," I said, giving her a way to justify what she wanted without losing face. I added the *please* because now that we'd started this dance, I didn't think I could bear for it to end without seeing her come, watching her surrender to her body's pleasure.

She nodded and then she started to move. Hard and fast or smooth and slow—I had no idea. There wasn't a force strong enough on the earth to make me look away from her eyes while she touched herself. As I watched, her cheeks colored and her lips parted, but it was to make space for her shallow breaths, not an attempt to draw me in. Or at least not *solely* an attempt to draw me in. I didn't doubt that my witness added to her arousal. I kept her foot caged between my hands, not caressing, more providing a physical reminder of my presence while she touched herself.

Her breathing came faster and I felt her foot flex against my palm but she didn't close her eyes. Not until the very last moment when her climax rolled over her. Her back arched and her body tightened like a bow string, the muscles of her calf bunching against my thigh. Her lips formed a perfect *O* as she breathed through her climax and her face and body went slack. When she opened her eyes again, it was as if I was seeing her for the first time, as if in that brief, unguarded second I caught a glimpse of her soul. It was more addictive than any drug, and I didn't know how long I'd be able to wait for my next hit.

I reached for her hand and it took me a few seconds to realize the car stopped. I'd been so lost in her pleasure, I had no idea how long we'd been sitting there. My driver had been with me long enough to know not to open the door until I signaled we were ready. Leaning toward her, I brought her fingers to my mouth and sucked them clean, tasting her slightly salty, tangy essence. Her chest hitched as her breath caught and I didn't have to tell her how much I wanted her. She knew.

"Thank you," I said, needing to be clear her sharing herself mattered more to me than any quick fuck.

She nodded, her eyes so wide and bright, still so open in the dimly lit car that for a moment I considered asking the driver to take us straight to my place, but I didn't trust myself to hold back when we were really alone. To me, dominance had always been about using the power my partner trusted me with for the pleasure of both of us. Alexandra would feel more pleasure, deeper pleasure when she really let go and trusted someone else to hold her. That meant not letting her fall into old patterns of performing for power. Which meant—for now at least— no sex. Until I could be sure I could be alone with her and not give in to the aching need to cover her with my body and fill her with my cock, we'd have to stick to sharing other only slightly less pleasurable things together.

"Come on, beautiful," I said, straightening her skirt for her. "We're late for tea."

I SAT ON the low bench, grateful this wasn't one of those tea places where you had to sit on the floor. My skirt would have made it impossible and after what happened in the back of Erik's car, I didn't trust my legs to support me if I gave in to their urge to crumple. Hell, I was so shaky, I'd needed his help to get into the shop. This time when he put his hand on the small of my back to guide me, it had been a necessity and not for show. It took every bit of my self-control to keep from leaning back against him, letting his body curve around me and support me. I still wanted that—to give in to his strength for just a few moments. To surrender to him.

It was insane. I'd been in lots more vulnerable positions with clients before. But I didn't come with them. I faked, very convincingly if I must say so myself, but letting go enough to actually orgasm? That was something I did in the safety of my own space, deep inside my own fantasies.

Erik pushed me to reveal more of myself than I ever intended, and I felt more vulnerable getting myself off with him next to me than I'd ever felt during sex. There'd been a moment after I climaxed when it felt like we connected on a deeper level, even though he barely touched me. And then he slid my fingers into his hot mouth, and any satisfaction I'd been feeling got burned away by how much I wanted him. It felt like going from zero to sixty in a flash of his dark eyes, as if my orgasm never happened, and I was thrown right back neck-deep into wanting him. Except this time nothing would make the feeling go away but him. Which was damned inconvenient, given how much energy I'd been expending trying to convince both of us that he didn't matter to me.

"Have you ever made tea using a Gaiwan before?" The diminutive man who appeared part Asian, part something else, and every bit of eighty years old sat in the chair opposite us and waited for my answer.

I thought of about a half dozen smart-ass Lipton comments but found I didn't want to say any of them. The tea shop was small—on scale with its proprietor—and smelled delicious, spicy, smoky, and herbal all at the same time. Glass apothecary jars holding dozens of kinds of teas lined the walls and I wanted to know what was in each of them. I was too curious to try to mask it with snark.

"No, sir. I'm not sure what a Gaiwan is, but I know I haven't used one."

"Good, good. You're going to love this. It's a completely different taste. Do you prefer green tea or black?"

The man directed the question at me. Our host greeted Erik when we arrived and the two of them shared a few words in a language I didn't understand but my companion had been silent ever since. Even after all my study, I guess a part of me still associated dominance with bossing someone around, but Erik managed to maintain complete control of the situation without saying a word. And instead of telling me what to do, I found myself wondering what he liked, what would please him. Even in his silence, or rather because of it, he was taking up an awful lot of space in my head.

I glanced over at him, but he simply smiled at me, a warm, steady presence, giving no indication which he preferred.

"Black, please," I said, opting for my favorite when faced with a vacuum.

"Very nice," said the man, rising with more ease than his apparent age should allow and going over to a collection of small jars on the far wall.

As I watched, he set a wooden tray—marked and polished smooth from what I assumed was years of use—on the counter. He lined up three unadorned white porcelain bowls on the tray and put a scoop from each jar into them.

"This one is pu-erh," he said, offering me the small bowl to smell.

I leaned in and inhaled the earthy, almost stringent aroma. Erik leaned in beside me and breathed in the scent, but he still didn't comment.

"I like that," I said, not sure whether I was supposed to wax on, like at a wine tasting. *Fruity but with a hint of bullshit or some such thing.*

Erik wasn't offering me any clues and the older man studied me like he was trying to fit me for a wand. At least I hadn't broken anything.

"This one is lapsang suchong," the man said, trading the bowl for the one next to it.

I breathed deep and struggled to keep from coughing. It smelled like tea that had been parked in a smoker for a day or two. I couldn't imagine brewing it would make any of that better.

"Are you okay?" Erik rested his hand, warm and strong, on my forearm, his touch firm through the silk of the blouse he'd chosen for me. My senses were compounding each other, everything threatening to overwhelm me. His touch, my body's reaction to him, the glide of fabric against my skin, the scents filling the space; I had no choice but to focus on the tea in front of me. If I thought about the man with the razor-sharp wit and kind eyes, I'd go over the edge. If I dwelt on the way he seemed to be trying to take care of me, I might not be able to climb out again.

"Maybe not that one," said the older man, setting the bowl down before picking up the next.

When he offered me the tea this time, I inhaled carefully, breathing in just a whiff at first. The slightly citrus scent of bergamot filled my nostrils, overlaid with something else. It was so subtle, it took me a moment to recognize the lavender. It had none of its normal soapy scent, just a delicate floral aroma that complemented the bergamot and rich tea. I smiled and breathed deeper, losing myself for a moment in the simple sensual pleasure of tea. Tea I hadn't even tasted yet.

"That's it. That's the one," said the man, taking away the tray and replacing the bowls with two tea cups and a low covered vessel that looked a little like a casserole dish.

He took a metal teapot off a burner in the corner and set everything on the table in front of us. If he went back for anything else, I was going to have to jump up and help. Nothing but the older man's appearance seemed frail, but it didn't seem fair to let the smallest of us do all the work.

"First we warm the Gaiwan." He poured a bit of steaming water into the casserole-looking thing, waiting a few moments before emptying it into a bowl.

Erik took my hand in both of his, cradling it in a touch that managed to be more tender than sexual. I glanced over and found him watching me with the same kind of intensity I'd been watching the tea-making process.

"Now we bloom the tea." The man took two big pinches of the dried leaves in his wrinkled fingers and dropped them into the white dish.

Gaiwan. I filed the word away to turn over in my head later. I loved learning new words. It was like finding interesting beads to string together.

He poured a small bit of water over the tea leaves and the heady aroma of bergamot grew stronger. Erik uncurled my fingers, cradling the back of my hand against his palm. Resting his thumb at the place where my pulse beat at my wrist, he traced the lines on my palm with his fingertips. My breath caught in my throat. It was nothing more than intense hand-holding, so why did it feel like his touch woke my whole body, making it bloom like the tea in front of us?

"Now that it's awake, we brew."

The old man filled the Gaiwan with hot water and covered it, but I was more focused on Erik's hands. I didn't know what *brewing* translated to in Erik's hand dance, but I'd never been a fan of public groping. I'd read too many of those forced orgasm stories to not assume Erik had a similar scene planned. The *don't let the waiter know you're coming while he reads you the specials* ones. As much as I wanted his hands on me—I could admit that much to myself—the idea of squirming in my seat opposite the tea-making man while Erik fingered me under the table didn't make the top twenty list of things I wanted to experience.

I tensed up, shifting slightly in my seat in case I needed to make a quick escape. My entire focus shifted from the tea brewing process in front of me to the man beside me, and I had the same predator/prey feeling from earlier. When he leaned in to press his lips to my ear, I couldn't hide the way I flinched.

"Relax, Alexandra." His breath felt hot against my ear, and I had the crazy push/pull desire to curl into the shelter of his body at the same time I wanted to move away. "I'm not going to do more than hold your hand. Pay attention so you remember the steps." He pitched his voice low enough that I was sure the older man didn't catch his actual words, if he was even paying that much attention to us. He seemed completely focused on the tea.

I nodded, shifting my attention back to the process in front of me, both grateful and disappointed when Erik leaned away.

"Now we decant."

Less than half a minute had passed, which seemed awfully quick to brew tea, but when the man poured the steaming liquid into the shallow bowls, it was a rich amber color. Erik let go of my hand and a sense of loss overwhelmed any relief I'd been feeling. I missed his touch the instant it was gone. He picked up his cup and waited for me to do the same before bringing it to his nose. I watched his chest expand out of the corner of my eye as he breathed in the scent. The handle-less cups were thin porcelain and the heat from the tea warmed my hands almost but not quite to the point of burning.

I held the cup for a moment, simply feeling the warmth transfer from the almost translucent clay to my palms and the place Erik had been touching me moments earlier. I didn't know whether I wanted the heat to burn away the sensation of his touch or call it back to life. Honestly, either was a lot to expect from a cup of tea. With the care the older man had taken making the tea, rushing to taste it felt wrong. Lifting the bowl, I inhaled and breathed in the rich scent. I took a moment to try to discern the different notes: the sharp scent of bergamot, the tannin-rich tea, and overtop of it all, the delicate clean floral of lavender.

I'd already experienced so much just from the process, tasting the rich amber liquid felt almost secondary. Until it hit my tongue and everything I'd been breathing in exploded in my mouth. I was never going to be able to look at good old Lipton the same way again.

"You can brew many cups from these leaves. Each will have its own taste and characteristic." He lifted the domed lid to show me the tea leaves, plumped up and dark-green/brown instead of the black they'd started as.

When he went to get the kettle of boiling water, Erik took my hand in his, bringing it to his lips to brush a kiss across the back of my fingers. The gesture was almost chivalrous, but it sent heat unfurling through me and for a moment I felt a kinship with the tea—blooming under his touch.

"THANK YOU FOR taking me there," I said three cups of tea later when we were back in Erik's car.

I felt like I might float away on a sea of tea, but I'd loved everything about the tiny shop and our host. I couldn't remember the last time I'd paid that kind of focused attention to such a simple task. The ritual changed everything—made it more important. It wasn't like I'd never experienced the power of ritual before. I grew up taking communion alongside everyone else in the Methodist church in the town I grew up in. I'd just never felt the shift from mundane to sacred quite as clearly. The man at the shop did more than brew tea. He turned the whole process into a kind of prayer.

"It was my pleasure," said Erik, sounding like he was talking about more than the tea lesson.

It was as if the man had a dial that let him turn up the heat between us with nothing but his voice, the same way the shop owner turned up the burner under the kettle. I was well on my way to scorching when Erik reached for my hand and resumed tracing the lifelines etched in my palm.

"Thinking of giving up law for fortune telling?" I had to do something to break the tension I felt building inside me. It was a classic smart-ass defense mechanism, but just because I realized it didn't mean I could do anything about it. I was afraid being too honest with Erik for too long might be dangerous for my mental health. Not that wisecracking like a sullen teenager was a much better stance.

"Some days there's not much separating the two. Both professions depend to a certain extent on performance."

And lying. I'd gone with some girlfriends in high school to see a fortune teller at the county fair. Madame

179

Zelda had promised me fame and academic acclaim. It's not the reason I'd gone the whole way for a PhD. I wasn't that fickle, but I'd thought about it over the years. The dusty incense-filled tent and the turbaned soothsayer spinning fairy tales that promised each of us exactly what we wanted and made a part of me believe I could have it. But Erik had been uncharacteristically nice. Calling him a liar seemed like a bad way to repay his effort, so I managed to hold my tongue.

He played with my fingers, stroking my hand and my desire—honestly, it was like the man had installed a link between my clit and my ring finger when I wasn't looking—as we headed downtown.

"So explain to me what today had to do with dominance and submission." Holding hands in the car felt too much like being on a date. It seemed prudent to drag things back to the reason we were spending time together.

"Today, Alexandra, is about you learning how to please me."

He said the words as if it were the most natural assumption in the world—that I'd care about his pleasure and want to be the one to please him. I opened my mouth to refute his claim and then shut it again. I actually did want to please him, which I have to say shocked the hell out of me. Maybe it was being raised to be the good girl. To be agreeable. But I didn't think so. That felt inauthentic. I shoved the thought into a box to look at later or to ignore if it messed too badly with my self-identity.

"And how would I go about doing that?" I swallowed hard, hoping he didn't hear the way my voice hitched and knowing he did. With his thumb pressed against my wrist, he'd feel my pulse hammering away. I could spin with the best of them, but I didn't stand a chance at pulling off disinterested with Erik. Not anymore. We'd gone too far for that.

"I'll show you when we get to my place."

ERIK

THE CAR MADE THE TURN off Canal and headed toward the Garden District. I tried to justify taking Alexandra to my house, but even I wasn't that good of a liar. *The club was too overtly sexual, her studio would make it too easy for her to fall into old patterns, I couldn't keep trying to feed her—the baby bird thing wouldn't work more than once with Alex. Honestly, it hadn't worked all that well the first time.* To varying degrees, it was all true. And a complete load of bullshit. I was taking her to my house because I wanted her there. I wanted to see what it felt like with her smart-ass energy filling my space, to smell the delicate floral of her perfume mixing with the sandalwood and sage scent of the old plantation house I'd inherited from my mother, who'd inherited it from husband number three.

"Are you sure we have time for whatever you've got planned? Don't you lawyers have to work all the time?"

Alexandra feigned disinterest and I smiled to myself. She clearly lived by the *best defense is a good offense* motto. The more nervous she got, the more bravado she wore. I could tell by the way her gaze tracked my movements and her pulse raced under my thumb that she was nervous.

"I can go back tonight to finish anything I need to. If you're worried about the length of our session, I'd be happy to pay for the extra time."

I had no trouble throwing money at problems, but we were going to have to come to some kind of resolution to the financial situation we were in. I wanted her submission willingly given, not paid for. And every time we traded money, we slid further into escort territory—a place I was pretty sure neither of us wanted to go.

"No, you have time left. You haven't exactly taxed me up to this point."

I caught and held her gaze, seeing what I hoped was anticipation in her eyes. She was nervous, but she was also interested. That was something I could work with.

"I'll see what I can do about that," I said and had the pleasure of watching her cheeks flush a rosy pink. Her skin blushed beautifully. I couldn't wait to color her ass with my hand.

"This is your house?" The disbelief in her tone dragged me away from the fucking spectacular image in my head, the one where she stretched out naked over my lap, her breasts bouncing against my thigh as I spanked her round ass.

"Not what you pictured?" I searched her profile as she leaned toward the window to take in the massive white painted façade with the two-story-tall Doric columns flanking the entrance.

I could appreciate the beauty of the majestic old house but even after all these years, it still didn't feel like home. I'd never lived there with my mother. I'd been off to law school by the time my mother married number three. His family was part of the old South, and the house had been in his family since before the Civil War. I think my mother loved the house more than she loved him, but they seemed happy together, on the surface at least. My mother rarely went deeper than that with anything. Unlike my father and husband number one, the last guy had been good to her and that's all I'd had to care about anyway.

When he'd died and she followed, the big old house had come to me. It was when I was up for partner and the grandeur of the place became another prop for me to use. It looked like the home of a partner in one of the most important law firms in New Orleans. I'd taken on the house the same way I donned my custom-made suits, playing the role until it was mine.

"I guess I'd assumed you were more of a modern loft kind of guy. This is so beautiful. When I first moved to the city, I used to walk from Magazine to St. Charles, looking at all the gorgeous houses and wondering what kind of people actually lived there. I'd never have guessed it was you." She smiled over her shoulder at me and despite her credulity—hell, maybe because of it—her enthusiasm was contagious.

"Come on. I'll give you a tour."

I opened my door and hurried around to her side of the car, waving away the driver when I got there. It was suddenly very important for me to be the one to help her out of the car and lead her to my front door.

I wanted to see her reaction to my space. I rarely brought women I was seriously interested in there. I'd rarely been seriously interested in a woman, so it wasn't exactly a hardship. Not until Julie and no one since.

"I don't suppose you've ever considered opening the house up for the Garden District Home Tour, have you?"

"Good Lord, no."

The last thing I wanted was a stream of strangers parading through my home, even if it was for a good cause. I'd much rather write a sizeable check and be done with it. Disappointment shaped her expression and I wondered why she cared so much. Before I could ask, the look was gone and we only had one room left. It was the spare bedroom I'd converted into a playroom back when I still thought Julie and I would be able to make things work.

The room was small—nothing of the scale of Alex's studio—and intimate. Although I wasn't sure if that was inherent to the space or my history with it. Up until that moment, I hadn't thought about sharing it with anyone else. The few times I'd played recently had been at Bacchus. I expected to connect the space with Julie and shocked the hell out of myself when I didn't. I debated not showing the space to Alex, but I wanted to see her reaction. To see if she'd blush again.

"I'm not sure how I'd explain this to the organizers," I said, keying in the entry code and ushering her into the room.

I studied her as her gaze took in the deep-blue walls and dark furnishings made up of a rough wooden St. Andrew's Cross and padded bench. Alex wrapped her hand around the square stock of the four-poster bed I'd had custom made for the space. Its sturdy frame and hidden rings offered all kinds of opportunities and I started picturing the way Alex would look stretched out for me across the silver-blue comforter.

I watched as she moved around the room, her fingers tracing the wood. She was a chameleon for so much of the time, only showing what she intended to project, but in less guarded moments, she wore her thoughts and feelings on her face for anyone willing to pay attention to see. I planned to pay attention to everything where Alex was concerned.

"You could always leave the door locked. They let owners do that when they don't want people in certain rooms."

It took me a second to realize she was talking about the home tour again. It didn't make sense. As far as I knew, she didn't have any connection with the Historical Society.

"I'm not interested in having my house included on the tour, Alex."

"You might change your mind."

"I won't," I said, holding the door to the hallway open for her.

"You don't want to stay in here?"

Her forehead creased down the center, and I let go of the door for a moment to step closer to her. Her eyes were wide and uncharacteristically unsure. I could see the pulse racing at the base of her throat.

"Want has nothing to do with it," I said, invading her space until she had to decide whether to take a step back or press her body against mine.

I felt her breasts skim my chest, her nipples hard peaks under the delicate silk and lace. She wanted me. She wanted this. However it may have started out, it wasn't about the money or the challenge anymore. This thing—whatever we decided to call it—was already about much more than that. I smoothed my thumb over the line in her forehead and watched her brown eyes go dark.

"I *want* to strip off your clothes, stretch your naked body out on the St. Andrew's Cross and take a leather-tipped cat to your ass until you're so wet, your thighs glisten. I *want* to suck your nipples so hard they stretch to tight peaks, perfect for me to attach clips to and then I *want* to work your belly and thighs over with the flogger until every inch of your skin comes to life. I *want* to pull the clips off with my teeth and suckle your aching nipples while I finger fuck you to your third or fourth orgasm. I *want* to make you come so many times you get hoarse from screaming my name."

Her eyes were dilated, and I could see her chest rise and fall with each shallow breath she took. She licked her lips and only my resolve not to let her top from the bottom kept me from tugging it between my teeth and catching her needy little cries with my mouth while I gave us both what we needed.

"Why don't you?" Her voice trembled but the set of her shoulders was more of a dare than a submission. "We seem to spend a lot more time talking than naked."

"It's going to stay that way until you understand—really understand—that you have all the power in this exchange. None of this means anything until you can actually surrender to me. Not for money and not on a dare. Not because you're weak. I know you're not. You need to have power to give it. Because you trust me to take the power you give me and use it for both of our pleasure." I ran a hand through my hair, not bothering to hide my frustration. My cock was so hard it ached. Painting the picture for her with my words had affected me as much, if not more. I wanted her with a hunger that bordered on desperation. But I knew from experience anything other than genuine surrender would leave me less satisfied than if I never touched her.

"I'm scared."

"I know, beautiful. That's part of the point. Anything real that exposes that much of your soul is scary, but it's also worth it. I'm not going to push. Not yet. Not until you're certain you can be honest with both of us." I cupped her face, loving the way she turned in to my touch, resting her cheek against my palm. "We'll get there. Don't worry."

"I was just…" She let the rest of what she'd been about to say fall away.

I tipped up her chin, forcing her to meet my gaze. "Just what, Alexandra?"

"Never mind. I'm curious; that's all."

"That's honest. What are you curious about?" My cock throbbed against the zipper of my too-tight slacks. I swear to God, I was tempted to step out for a moment to jerk off and relieve some of the pressure so I could actually think clearly. But I had a feeling nothing would change the state of my cock as long as Alex was in my house.

"About the flogger." She swallowed, and I forced my focus to stay on her eyes and not her gorgeous lips. "I've never had anyone who actually knew what they were doing use a flogger. On me."

Fuck me.

"And you've decided I do?" I called on every bit of training I had to keep from letting my emotions influence what she was telling me. Which was fucking impossible, given how much I wanted what I thought she was offering me.

"With the way you've been able to mind fuck me using nothing more than your voice, a tie and some tea? Yes, I'm pretty sure you know your way around a flogger. I can't promise I'll be any good at submitting, but I can promise to be honest with you and to try. I want to try."

I debated for a fraction of a second as I watched the emotions play across her beautiful face. This woman pushed me past the point of reason. My limits didn't seem to matter where she was concerned. It was the glimpse of curiosity and, even more, the hope I saw in her expression that made the decision for me. I took a step back and let my gaze trace a path from her face to her toes and back again. By the time I reached her eyes again, her lips were parted and her cheeks flushed.

"Strip, Alexandra."

Alex

I'D DONE MORE THAN POKE the sleeping tiger this time. I'd opened his jaws and put my tastiest bits inside his mouth, and I couldn't find the self-preservation to regret any of it.

As I reached for the buttons on my blouse, I had to fight to keep my hands from shaking. Taking off my clothes was supposed to be the easy part. I'd already done it for him once before so why did I feel so nervous?

"Start with your shoes, Alexandra." Erik studied me from a few steps away, his arms crossed in front of him, making the neckline of his pale-gray shirt gap.

He hadn't worn a tie—just the dress shirt and charcoal slacks—and under other circumstances, I'd relish the glimpse of his chest the open collar gave me. Or I would if my brain wasn't stuttering over his words. Taking off my shoes should be the simplest thing in the world. Hell, you can do that kind of thing in front of anyone, but my mind was already spinning ahead to what came after.

I'd spent more than my fair share of time naked in front of men but it had always been with an element of performance. I stripped to entice, starting with my blouse and ending with my shoes and with each piece I removed, my power grew. Standing naked or mostly naked in my heels while I watched the man in front of me wrestle with lack of blood flow to his brain was something I was very comfortable with. Taking off my shoes and then my clothes wouldn't be stripping; it would be baring myself. Making myself vulnerable instead of being the one gaining the upper hand with each stitch of clothing.

"Use your safe word if you want to stop. Otherwise, take off your shoes. Now." Erik pinned me with his gaze, holding me in place with nothing more than his command and his eyes glued to mine. I had no doubt he knew exactly what he was doing to me and that's exactly why he was doing it.

No way was I going to use my safe word over a pair of shoes. I toed off my pumps, grimacing as I dropped four inches in height.

"Good girl."

I rolled my eyes at him as I curled my toes into the incredibly soft carpet. Instead of the *behave or I'll punish you* bullshit I expected, he laughed, a deep, throaty chuckle that warmed me from the inside.

"Skirt." He relaxed his stance and waited for me to comply. *As if there were any doubt.*

I reached around to the small of my back to unzip the skirt and felt the fabric of my blouse drag over my aching breasts. Even covered in lace, they were so sensitive I was afraid by the time Erik actually got around to touching me, I might self-combust. I wanted this— wanted him so much; it made it difficult to breathe. Shimmying the skirt over my hips, I let it drop to the floor and stepped out of it.

"Leave it," he said when I started to bend to pick it up.

I had no trouble obeying that command. Without my panties—even crazier, without my shoes—I felt bare. Exposed. Vulnerable.

"Thank you for trusting me." He took a step toward me and my pulse kicked up a notch. Or a hundred.

When he reached for the buttons on my blouse, I could barely hear over the whooshing of my heartbeat hammering in my ear. With fingers steadier than mine, Erik made quick work of the blouse, sliding the silk over my shoulders without ever really touching me.

"Turn around."

I did, grateful for a chance to hide, if just for a moment. With every moment we spent together in that room and every inch of my skin he bared, this thing between us became more real. I wasn't pretending to submit or to make myself vulnerable. I was willingly surrendering control to him. I closed my eyes for a moment, afraid the honesty would overwhelm me. I didn't want to quit but I didn't know how to keep going, so I waited for him to tell me what to do.

His fingers brushed my back as he unfastened the clasp on my bra. So desperate for his touch, I had to fight the urge to curl into him, to demand his hands on my skin. But this time wasn't about demanding. It was about giving and accepting, about learning my limits and about trust and honesty, so I stilled myself with uncharacteristic patience and waited for the scrap of lace to fall away, leaving me completely exposed.

Goose bumps pebbled my flesh, and my nipples tightened to impossibly hard peaks, but I stayed still, frozen in place, waiting for Erik's next instruction. He moved away from me, and I didn't turn around. I didn't trust myself to—not and be able to maintain any semblance of control. I heard the slide of a drawer and my mind shot to the nipple clamps he'd pocketed from my studio. The ones I'd never had the nerve to try with anyone before.

My body was strung tight as a bow, and I felt myself tremble. He'd see it, see the tremors moving through me in anticipation of his touch, and he'd know he was the cause, but there wasn't a thing I could do about it. Unless I was willing to end things, I had no choice but to wait for him to show me what he wanted from me. He gathered my hair together in a thick ponytail before sectioning it and making quick work of plaiting it. I felt him tug the end and heard the snap of an elastic band and then he stepped back again, letting the braid fall against my back.

"Turn around."

The low command should be nothing, the easiest thing in the world, but when I turned, I'd be facing him. He'd be able to look into my eyes and then there really wouldn't be anywhere to hide. I inhaled, hating the way my breath fluttered and loving it at the same time. I turned.

"My God, you're beautiful." Erik said the words as if they were more than a compliment, as if they were something deeper, something sacred. He tipped my chin up with his fingers, forcing me to meet his gaze.

I fought the urge to blink. To try to hide. And then my gaze met his and I fell into his whiskey-colored eyes, lost myself in the honest appreciation I saw and the surety that whatever happened, this man wouldn't let me fall. He was strong enough to hold me when I needed it.

"I don't know what to do." I paused, not sure how to explain my feelings.

"It's okay, sweetheart. I do."

The certainty in his response washed over me, and I let out a shaky breath. *This man.* This man was strong enough to master me. I didn't know if I was strong enough to let go, but I wanted to be.

"I'm going to give you a choice. I wouldn't normally, but nothing about this is normal for me."

He reached forward and cupped my cheek, the tenderness made more powerful by the fact that I was naked in front of him. Bared for our mutual pleasure.

"Usually we'd have worked our way up to the flogger. By the time we got there, I'd know exactly what you needed. Since this is our starting point, you can decide whether you want to be bound or whether you trust yourself to be able to hold still." He searched my face, and I swallowed, but didn't hide. "Choose, beautiful." His thumb brushed my bottom lip and my mouth parted in anticipation.

I didn't have to think about it. It wasn't even close. Despite the amount of time I spent tied up, I'd never really been bound before. I'd never given over that kind of control to anyone. I wanted to give it to him.

"Bind me. Please."

ERIK

THIS WOMAN PUSHED every boundary I had. Every time I thought I knew what I was doing, she knocked me sideways. In the beginning, it had been like playing chess, anticipating her reactions and trying to outmaneuver her. And I'd loved it, loved the challenge of trying to figure out how to make her feel or watching her give in to the pleasure. This was so much more.

The more I pushed for her honesty and surrender, the more I had to give of my own. It was as if we were scaling a cliff together, each of us pushing the other on as the ledge narrowed in front of us. Instead of calling uncle, she kept walking closer to the razor slice of the edge, leaving me no choice but to follow or be left behind. No way in hell would I let that happen. I would be the one to hold her when she flew. I'd be the one to keep her safe and pray she didn't steal my heart in the process.

Taking her hand, I led her over to the fixed ring in the corner of the room. I'd thought about positioning her on the cross but I wanted access to all of her. The ring gave me that. She was noticeably shorter without her heels and her hand felt small and delicate in my much larger one. All of it added to the contrast between us. Rough—soft. Large—small. Naked—clothed. It should have included vulnerable and in control but I had a feeling that would never be the case with Alex. The best I could hope for was both of us vulnerable.

"Arms up, sweetheart."

She hesitated, and for a moment the uncertainty was etched on her beautiful face. She wanted this—she'd been the one to ask for it—but she was scared too. *Of the experience or herself? Both maybe.* It didn't matter. I could take care of her. I *wanted* to take care of her. Wrapping my hands around her ribcage, I slid my palms over her skin, skimming the sides of her breasts and pressing higher until she raised her arms. I ran my hands up her arms, urging her hands higher until her palms met above her head and I could cuff her wrists with my hands.

I wanted to touch her everywhere, to run my hands over every inch of her skin and feel her tremble under my fingertips. I'd waited this long; I could wait a few moments more. But just a few.

"Stay still," I said, holding her gaze as I let go of her wrists and reached for the cable attached to the ring.

Focusing on the task in front of me instead of watching the way her gorgeous breasts moved as she inhaled, I fastened a wide padded Velcro cuff to each wrist and clipped them together to the cable, leaving a bit of slack.

"Still with me?"

She nodded, her lips parted and her eyes wide.

"Good." I took a few steps away and grabbed a spreader bar and a soft suede flogger from the cabinet. "Feet shoulder width apart." It was the reason I'd left slack in the line. When I had her completely bound, I wanted her stretched tight and still standing but supported by the cable so she didn't have to think about anything but the kiss of the leather against her skin.

Keeping her gaze fixed to the leather toy, Alex took a tentative step, spreading her legs a few inches.

"That's not what I told you," I said, clicking the bar in my hands a notch wider. I set the flogger to the side and held the bar in front of me. "I'll keep going until you comply, beautiful. It extends to four feet."

I tipped my head as if it didn't matter either way to me. It did. I wanted her submission voluntarily given, not under threat of punishment. Not this time anyway.

I didn't have to wait long. She widened her stance and I dropped to my knees in front of her, which put her sweet sex in front of my face and re-ordered my priorities. I blew across her bare mound and watched the muscles in her legs tighten as she strained to stay still.

"Don't you dare move." I looked up at her from my position between her spread legs and waited for her to nod her agreement.

I fastened the cuffs on the bar to her ankles with a speed that would have done an Indy pit crew proud and then I gripped her hips with my hands and gave in to what I'd been wanting to do since the first moment I held her in my arms. Spreading her labia with my thumbs, I wrapped my lips around her swollen clit and sucked hard. Her legs tensed and her back bowed as if she'd been shocked. I heard the clink and rattle as she pulled against the cable holding her arms. I kept up a steady pulsing pressure, drawing her clit into my mouth and teasing her with the scrape of my teeth against her tender flesh.

"Please. God. Fuck. Erik. Fuck."

The words fell from her lips in a steady stream as her body tensed and writhed under my hands and mouth. I hadn't intended to go straight for the orgasm. I'd meant to do a slow buildup, to make her beg for me to take her over the edge. But like every plan I'd made where Alex was concerned, she'd blown right through it. I'd just meant to take a taste but her response to my touch made it impossible for me to stop. Not until I made her come.

Tightening my grip on her hip with one hand because *I* needed the anchor this time, I slid two fingers through her slick folds and teased her opening. She was so fucking wet. Knowing I was the one who made her body respond was the fucking greatest thing ever. My cock was so hard it ached and each needy little cry made me that much harder.

"Please. Oh God. Please."

She rocked her hips forward as much as the bonds would let her. Grinning, my lips still pressed to her clit, I gave her what she needed. I thrust two fingers deep inside her and curled them toward the front of her body while I kept a steady pressure on her clit with my lips and tongue. It took moments, as if she'd been hanging on the edge for days—the same edge I was hanging on—waiting for me to touch her, and then she was coming, her body shaking as her pussy pulsed and tightened around my fingers.

Resting my forehead against the soft swell of her stomach, I pressed a kiss to her bare mound and gave us both a minute to catch our breath.

"That was unexpected," she said, and I smiled at the truth in her words. "I can't believe I finished so fast."

Standing on legs shakier than I was comfortable admitting, I nuzzled her neck and pressed a kiss behind her ear.

"Oh, beautiful," I said, reaching for the flogger. "We're not even close to finished."

MY BODY STILL trembled with the aftershocks of my climax as Erik circled me, looking like a lion ready to pounce. Which made me the stupid gazelle, tied up and at the big cat's mercy. Except Eric wasn't a lion, and I'd asked for this. I wanted this. His mouth on my clit shot to the top of my favorite things list. Honestly, I'd expected to have to beg before he'd let me come, and I would have. I do just about anything to get him to touch me, to put his mouth on me again. His cock inside me.

"I assume you know the basic premise of pain and endorphin levels?" He held the grip of the flogger in one hand and ran the tails through the fingers of his other hand, as comfortable as if the leather was part of his body.

"The body releases endorphins in response to sensations normally perceived as painful, resulting in a morphine-like effect. Endorphins are dumped into the blood stream all at once in a load. It requires ten minutes for the endorphin load to build up and be released." I swallowed hard. It was one thing to read a bunch of statistics. It was another thing entirely when faced with the business end of a flogger wielded by someone who knew how to use it. Unlike my timid client, I had no doubt Erik knew exactly what he was doing. I'd been fascinated with the idea of sub space since I came across it in my research. I'd just never trusted anyone enough to take me there. I trusted Erik.

"That's right, but it's more than that," said Erik, circling closer.

I tracked him, every nerve in my body on high alert as I waited for him to strike. No fucking pun intended.

"The key is to keep ramping up the endorphin loads so they compound each other. After the first ten minutes, a sub's experience of pain as well as their threshold shifts." He circled me, trailing the flogger between his hands, capturing my attention completely. "An experienced Dom can help their sub reach such a heightened state of arousal, stimuli that would normally be experienced as discomfort or pain become one more layer of potential pleasure."

He moved the hand holding the flogger closer to me, and I sucked in a breath in anticipation. But instead of flicking me with the tails, he brushed the back of his fingers over my breast, circling but not quite touching my areola.

"Every stimulus is perceived as an experience to move toward," he said, running the back of his hand over the tight peak of my nipple.

I pulled against the bounds holding my wrists and arched my back, desperate for more. He stroked my aching nipple again and then twisted his wrist so the leather tails kissed the side of my breast. I sucked in a breath and held it as he repeated the movement, a little harder this time, with a bit more sting. One, two, three more times he brought the tails down gently on my breast. Always around but never on my nipple until all I could think about was what it would feel like to have the leather touch me there.

"Every touch, every small bite of pain adds to the sensations, driving you higher."

He flicked his wrist and the tails struck my nipple with a sting. Before I could catch my breath, he struck again with more bite this time, hard enough that I couldn't swallow my gasp. And then his mouth was on me, suckling my abused flesh, drawing my nipple deeper into his mouth. Soothing me with his tongue.

It was as if my brain shifted direction in a split second and I couldn't make sense of anything—couldn't think anything but more. I wanted more. I let out the breath I'd been holding and relaxed in the tender ministrations of his lips on my nipple. When he bit gently, his teeth ringing my nipple, I pressed into him. It would shock the hell out of me later, but in the moment—deep in the moment—the only words that filtered through my brain were single-syllable pleas. *More. Yes. Fuck. Please. God.*

"That's it, beautiful. Just like that." He circled again, punctuating his praise with intermittent strikes of the leather against my skin.

The blows landed on my butt, my ribcage, the underside of my breasts. He tickled the place where my spread thighs met my ass and my world narrowed focus to the points of leather touching my skin. Kissing. Biting. Dull thuds and stinging caresses. I lost track of time, lost track of everything but Erik and the way he made me feel.

"Still with me, sweetheart?" He held my face in his hand, forcing me to meet his gaze and momentarily pulling me out of the buzzing, vibrating mess he'd made of my nerves.

"Yes. I want…" The words came out as a whisper and I couldn't figure out how to finish the sentence.

"I know." He kissed me, and I opened for him willingly or unable to deny him anything.

I knew with a soul-deep certainty, trusting Erik completely was the only reason I could surrender. I'd never be able to give myself over to the sensations he wove over my body like a tapestry if I didn't know without a doubt that he was man enough to hold me. To keep me safe while I flew.

Fuck. The thought should terrify me. Before the idea could take root, he broke the kiss and brought the leather tails down on my ass with enough bite to make me tug against my bonds. Then it was a light kiss of leather over my ribcage. A sting of tails against my nipple and his mouth there to soothe the sting before it even registered. My sex wept for him, arousal painting my thighs. I whimpered—desperate, hungry, needy little cries falling from my lips in an incoherent string.

The tails snapped against my aching, swollen clit and my body bucked, a combination of needing to close my legs and to bring him closer at the same time. He struck again—not hard—but the stinging kiss of leather hit its mark. Someone screamed, a high keening cry but I couldn't think of anything but the climax pushing me closer and closer to the edge. I was going over. I couldn't stop, and I didn't know if I'd survive it.

Erik dropped to his knees in front of me, wrapped his lips around my abused clit and sucked. His fingers filled me, ripping the orgasm from my body, and I shattered with the pleasure of it. Flying free.

16

ERIK

ALEX SUBMITTED TO ME THE way she did everything—with her whole self. Once she'd made the decision to give herself to me, she hadn't held anything back. Her vulnerability ripped through my heart and demanded I meet her with the same level of honesty. Which scared the shit out of me. Never mind that I'd been the one to push us down this path to begin with.

"You were so brave, sweetheart." I folded her in the soft blanket and hoisted her into my arms. I needed to hold her—to catch my breath while I took care of her and scrambled to make sure I maintained some semblance of control. She'd done her part. The last thing I wanted to do was to let her down because my emotions suddenly decided to get in the way. "So open, so beautiful. Thank you for your trust."

I murmured the words against the top of her head as I carried her out of the playroom to the sofa in the sitting room. I wanted a chance to hold her for as long as she'd let me and the sofa would give us enough room for me to wrap myself around her. It's the place I'd intended to bring her before she derailed my plans for the second time that day. None of that mattered now. I wouldn't change a moment of what happened between us. Her arms wrapped around my neck as she curled against me, using my body as her shelter, was the sweetest gift she could have given. This gorgeous, powerful creature trusted me enough to give up control, to let me take us where we both needed to go. Understanding that kind of exchange was heady business, but there was an extra layer with Alex. One I'd never felt before, not even with Julie. Maybe especially not with Julie. I was afraid now that I'd felt it, I would never be satisfied with less again.

I didn't even feel the strain as I carried her down the stairs to the sitting room. I could have walked for miles with her in my arms if I'd needed to and never felt the fatigue. I paused to snag a bottle of water to go with the chocolate I grabbed before we left the playroom. She shifted and I squeezed tighter, needing her to know that I had her.

"I don't need you to carry me. I can walk." She squirmed against me, and I pressed my lips to the top of her head.

"I need it, beautiful. Humor me for a few moments longer."

Still holding her in my arms, I relaxed against the leather, moving until I could settle her between my legs and pull her back to rest her head against my chest.

"Sip." I held the bottle of water to her lips and waited for her to drink. "Now this." I held up a square of dark chocolate and waited for her to open her mouth so I could place it on her tongue. She let out a groan of pleasure and my already hard cock twitched in response, as if she had some kind of remote control for my body. It was the opposite of the way it was supposed to work. I was the one who was supposed to control her responses. Nothing about this woman fit my preconceived ideas.

"Mind-blowing orgasms and chocolate. What's not to love?" The smart-ass was back in her tone, but her voice held enough of a tremor to let me know she hadn't fully recovered.

Good. I sure as hell hadn't recovered yet.

The constant state of arousal—scratch that, the fucking ache in my perpetually hard cock—was nothing compared to the number she'd done on my heart. No way in hell would I name what I felt but I couldn't deny it either.

"Again." I held the water bottle to her lips and waited for her to take a swallow.

"You're doing the baby bird thing again."

"Your point?"

I could practically see the gears turning behind her eyes. The woman was wide open, and her thoughts and emotions played like a movie across her beautiful face.

"No point. Just an observation."

I broke off another bite of chocolate and held it out for her, nestling her tighter in my arms when she took it from my fingers.

"How are you feeling?" I was pretty sure she'd want to dissect every single thing we'd done, but that could wait until later. Much later. Right now I just wanted to hold her and make sure she was okay. Hell, better than okay. I wanted her to feel fucking amazing.

"Spectacular. Really, truly spectacular."

She squirmed around a bit on my lap and I fought to hide my grimace as she wriggled against my aching cock. We'd gotten so much farther than I'd expected. Far enough that I'd considered loosening the cable so I could bend her over and sink balls-deep into her hot pussy. I'd crossed every other boundary I'd set for myself or moved it out of the way. What was one more?

In the end, I'm not sure what stopped me. There really wasn't anything that scared me. I met challenges head on and worked my way through them. But taking that final step, claiming her like that, felt like walking off the side of a cliff into thin air. I wasn't sure what I'd do if she slipped back into old sex-for-power habits. It seemed safer not to take the chance, which was all kinds of fucked up. Taking chances was what I did.

"Good, beautiful. Just relax." I pressed my lips against the top of her head and stroked her hair, content to have her drift off in my arms.

"But we're not done." Pulling out of my grip, she sat up and turned to face me. "You didn't come."

That was the understatement of the century. Between her squirming and the glimpses of her gorgeous skin flushed pink from my ministrations, it would be a miracle if I didn't go off in my pants like a horny teenager.

"That's not what this was about. It's okay," I added, smoothing the wrinkle in the center of her forehead with my thumb.

"No, it's not."

She let the blanket fall open but I didn't think it was some kind of attempt at a power grab. She seemed too focused on my response to realize she'd offered me a glimpse at her breasts topped with nipples I couldn't wait to get my mouth on again. I reached out to touch a finger to the pebbled tip, and she sucked in a breath, glancing down at my hand and confirming my assumption.

"I want you to come too."

Fuck, the woman was going to kill me. My best-laid plans were no match for the determination burning in her eyes. I was already well acquainted with her tenacity.

"I will. Just not right now. We took big steps today. Bigger than I intended. I want a chance to do it all again and so much more." I met and held her gaze, willing her to hear the truth in my words. "You're not ready for me to fuck you. Don't worry, we'll get there."

I recognized my mistake the instant the words left my mouth. It was like waving a red cape in front of a bullfighter. I braced myself for the fight I knew was sure to follow, but instead of attacking, she rolled her eyes.

"Oh please. I'm not ready for you to fuck me?" She cut her eyes in my direction, and I made a calculated decision to wait her out.

There was nothing I could think of to say that would make the situation any better and lots of things that could add to the current clusterfuck.

"Fine," she said, letting the blanket fall from her shoulders and baring her body to me. "No cock-in-pussy sex today. There are other ways to make you come."

"Such a filthy mouth." The crude language from someone who spent so much time in her head had an extra punch, and I clenched my fists to keep from hauling her over to straddle my lap.

"That's what I said." She scooted to the edge of the sofa and slid to her knees in front of me, reaching for my belt.

If I was going to stop her, I had to move now. We were screaming past the point of no return. Once she got her mouth on me, I was done. I gripped the hand working at my zipper.

"Stop thinking so loud, Counselor. You're going to give us both headaches." She paused in her attempts to open my fly and looked up at me, her dark eyes clear and warm. "Please, Erik. I want to do this. I need it."

There was a better than average chance I'd never be able to deny this woman anything. She always seemed to find a way around my limits, regardless of where I set them.

"Fine. It's a hardship, but if you insist," I said, releasing her hand.

She bit me through the fabric of my slacks, sinking her sharp teeth into my inner thigh. I hissed in a breath, and she blinked up at me, innocence personified, if innocence was a sex kitten with a wicked mouth and even wickeder mind.

"I forgot. It's important for the subject to be fully aroused in order for the pain to be experienced as something to move toward, right?"

"Brat." I opened my mouth to say something else but before I got the words out, her hand slid under the elastic of my boxer briefs. She wrapped her fingers around my still hard cock, sending the last of my blood flow away from my brain.

"You love me, admit it." She froze for a second as if she'd just realized what she said.

I had an instant to wonder whether she meant it or whether she was being a smart ass and then she wrapped her gorgeous lips around my cock, and I couldn't think of anything but *get more of her. All of her as close as I could fucking get.*

Alex slid down my length, taking me deep in her mouth until her nose bumped against my stomach. Hollowing her cheeks, she pulled back, holding just the head of my cock with her lips. Cupping my balls with her other hand, she repeated the movement, taking me into her wet heat and then sucking hard as she pulled away. I reached for her, grabbing her thick braid and twisting it around my fist as much to keep from choking her with my thrusting as it was to bring her closer. She picked up the rhythm, and I tightened my grip to slow her down. I didn't want to rush to the end and I was so close; it was a miracle I'd lasted this long. She ran her tongue up my length and I tugged her hair hard enough to make her let out a throaty moan.

"Fuck, beautiful. That feels so good." I glanced down and caught her watching me, eyes wide, with my cock filling her mouth. No calculation, nothing but pleasure in her gaze. That was all I could take, seeing her on her knees the way I'd imagined a thousand fucking times before. I was done. "Coming. God, I'm gonna come."

I tugged her ponytail, but instead of pulling back, she dug her fingers into my hips and took me as deep as she could. Straining against the feelings threatening to swamp me, I let go, painting the back of her throat as she swallowed everything I gave her. I couldn't admit it—I wouldn't—but with every barrier we broke through together, it was getting harder to deny the truth of her words. Whether she meant them or not.

Alex

"WHAT *DID* YOU plan to do with me? Cooking lessons? Soap making?" I said, teasing.

Sarcasm was the last bit of armor I had left. I'd exposed everything else to him. I needed to hold onto some kind of control. Although, I did have a better understanding of what he'd meant when he said the submissive was the one with the power. Surrendering to Erik had managed to be both humbling and liberating at the same time and so powerful. I was going to be working through my feelings about this for a long time. Not the least of which was the way my body responded to really being bound for a change—no quick release, easy out—by someone who knew what the hell he was doing and was strong enough to take care of both of us. The experience left me shaky, more than just physically. It shifted some of my long-held beliefs in a way I wasn't completely comfortable with.

"I'd planned to get you to read to me. Part of the Dom/sub relationship is about the submissive learning to please the dominant partner."

Keeping the blanket wrapped around my naked body—honestly, it was the softest thing I'd ever felt and my nerves were still hypersensitive—I leaned forward enough to look him in the eye. His grip on my hip tightened almost reflexively before relaxing again. I loved that he didn't seem to want to let me go almost as much as I hated moving out of the shelter of his arms, but I had to know where he was going with the *pleasing the Dom* thing. It didn't seem all that different than what a vanilla couple would do and if it was, I wasn't sure how I felt about it.

"I thought I did that a couple of minutes ago," I said, deliberately biting the corner of my lip.

Erik caught my chin with his hand, pressing his thumb against my bottom lip and holding me in place.

"You did. Please me very much," he said, his voice pitched low in a way that sent heat unfurling deep in my body and flooding my sex.

I shifted on the smooth leather cushion, squeezing my thighs together in a ridiculous effort to make my arousal less obvious. I don't know who the hell I thought I was fooling. I'd spent enough time with him to know Erik didn't have any trouble seeing right through me. It was like a bad *Star Trek-resistance is futile* kind of thing with orgasms at the end. That didn't mean I wasn't going to try.

"So what did you want me to read? Were you thinking a copy of the *Story of O* or do your tastes run more toward Michener or SCOTUS opinions?"

"Smart ass," he said, pinching my still tender nipple.

I yelped and felt my face flush with a mixture of embarrassment and arousal. I couldn't explain why the slight bite of pain did it for me, but I was done trying to deny it. After the way I shattered for him under the bite of the leather tails, he wouldn't believe it anyway. I could psychoanalyze the shit out of my responses later but for now I intended to enjoy the way Erik made my body feel. I'd worry about the rest another time.

"Since you handled the flogger so beautifully, I *was* going to let you off the hook." He punched the word in a

213

way that made it clear my smart-ass mouth put me firmly back on the hook.

Erik leaned toward me and I sucked in my breath in anticipation. Instead of touching me again, he reached past me to snag a well-worn paperback from a sweetgrass basket beside the sofa. He placed the book in my hands and relaxed back against the leather, looking like the king of the world. The complete self-assurance in his stance—like he knew whatever he commanded would happen—made my body tighten, but I managed to curtail the urge to roll my eyes.

Honesty, both about my feelings and about the way my body responded to him, was a hell of a lot harder than I expected. It was so much easier to go for the snark. I'd always been a basically truthful person. I prided myself on my integrity. I hadn't realized how much I lied, even about simple meaningless things, until Erik demanded my honesty. Not that orgasms were meaningless, not at all, but somewhere along the way it had gotten easier to simply smile and hide my genuine responses to things. Not my opinions, those I was perfectly comfortable sharing—hell, broadcasting if necessary—but my feelings were a different thing.

I didn't want them to be. I wanted to be as honest with my body and my heart as I was with my mind. Erik could help me with that. Although I had no intention of telling him. The irony wasn't lost on me. *Baby steps.* Needing a buffer between the thoughts in my head and the half-dressed would-be king radiating heat next to me, I glanced at the book in my hands.

"*Outlander*? You want me to read Diana Gabaldon's *Outlander* to you? It's like six hundred pages long." And one of my favorite books of all time but that didn't seem the salient point at the moment.

"You don't have to start at the beginning if you don't want to. My page is marked. Or we can start over, if you'd rather." For the first time in all time we'd spent together, Erik seemed—not unsure exactly; that would be too strong of a word—less than completely in control was probably more accurate. And he'd given me a choice.

My attention shifted with laser focus to what could possibly make him feel like that. It was, after all, a hell of a lot easier to analyze someone else's weaknesses than it was to look at my own. Although even thinking about weak and Erik in the same sentence felt disingenuous.

"You're a hundred and ten pages into the book," I said, flipping to the spot he'd marked. "Why would you want to start over? Why have me read to you at all?" Never mind for the moment, the fact that when the big bad attorney wanted to read, he picked a time-traveling historical romance.

"I like your voice," he said, as if it were the most obvious thing in the world. "I'm not expecting you to do the characters. Unless you want to." He gave me a cocky grin that made me want to strangle him and kiss him at the same time.

It was a toss-up which desire was stronger, and then his expression shifted to something less guarded and kissing edged out bodily harm.

"I'm dyslexic, Alex. I love the stories—the language—but I have to work so hard at reading; it takes the joy out of it for me."

I had about a million questions about how he got through law school with dyslexia. Hell, how he handled his daily life. It wasn't like he'd chosen a profession that didn't rely on the written word. Brevity with words was a legal oxymoron. Thinking about how hard he must have worked to get where he was tugged at my heart, making me care even more. The man never stopped surprising me.

"Alexandra," he said, using the same voice he'd used in the playroom earlier to get me to answer him. "I have an abundance of coping mechanisms I've developed over the years. I'd be happy to talk about them another time. I'm sure you have reams of questions, but we're done with this issue for now. Either use your safe word or read."

I hadn't considered the idea that we were still in a scene, and I wasn't sure how I felt about it—that he could just play the Dom card whenever he wanted. At some point, we were going to have to talk about where the line was, but it didn't have to be today.

Settling back into my spot against his chest, I opened the book to the first page and started to read.

"OH, AYE, SASSENACH, I AM your master…and you're mine. Seems I canna possess your soul without losing my own." I kept replaying the quote from *Outlander* in my head as I walked the last few blocks to the restaurant. I could almost feel Erik's strong arms holding me and his lips pressed to the top of my head as I read to him.

Actually, my entire time with Erik seemed to have etched itself on my psyche. Deeper, if I was being honest with myself, which I was making a concerted effort to do. If nothing else, being with Erik taught me how often I hid or suppressed my real feelings. I wasn't going to become one of those people who used the truth to bludgeon others, but I was going to do a better job being honest with myself. Starting with the fact that I loved the way Erik played my body, and that there might be something genuine to this dominance and submission thing.

Surrendering to him while he used the fine line between pleasure and pain to show me new, deeper sensations had been one of the most powerful experiences of my life. And I had a feeling we were just getting started. There was so much more he could teach me and so much more I wanted to know.

It shocked the hell out of me, but it wasn't just BDSM stuff. His dyslexia confession brought up a dozen more questions and made me want to understand him that much more. How crazy strong and committed did a person have to be to get through law school when they struggled to read? He'd shown me his text-to-voice app on his way to take me home and explained some of his coping methods. Everything he told me made me like him that much more. *Like* was the only *L* word I was even thinking, but I had to admit, the man was so much more than I'd first imagined. And I was getting in deeper every minute we spent together.

Pushing the uncomfortable thought aside, I opened the door to the raw food restaurant Elena had chosen for lunch. The interior was practically covered with Carrara marble. Everything was smooth and white, and the restaurant smelled like fresh cut grass and chamomile. It was the scent of every summer I'd had growing up except I had a feeling there wouldn't be any Nutty Buddy cones at the end of this meal.

I gave my name to the host and followed him to a table beside what looked like a back-lit Himalayan salt wall. I sat in the rosy glow and studied a menu full of food I didn't really want to eat. In a city known for its food, I still couldn't quite believe we were eating in a place that didn't even cook the food. I had to keep reminding myself that wasn't the point. It was Elena's choice. It felt a little like my friends were taking turns babysitting me. I tried to focus on feeling loved and not on the slightly helpless desperation that came from suddenly having no job and friends determined to keep me busy. I ordered a beet juice mocktail and relaxed back into the surprisingly comfortable seat to wait.

Elena blew in a few minutes past the hour, looking pretty if slightly frazzled, and I wondered what she had to move around to make time for me. I hated feeling like the weakest link. At least this time I might have something helpful to offer her.

"I'm so sorry," she said, taking my hand in hers and leaning in to kiss my cheeks. "I hope you haven't been waiting long."

"Not long at all." The drink I'd barely touched supported my statement. "I honestly understand if you don't have time for lunch." And it would mean I wouldn't be stuck pretending uncooked vegetables counted as food.

"Don't be silly. A client turned me on to this place. I love it here." The smile lit her face, which was a clear illustration of different strokes and all that.

The server took Elena's order for a green supreme juice, and we paused for a moment to glance at the menu. Oyster po' boy and fries hadn't sprouted up among the nuts and berries, so I settled on a zucchini wrap. At least it included avocado, which wasn't as good as bacon but better than wheatgrass. Elena had the same with the avocado and cashew sour cream on the side.

"Seriously?"

"I like it that way."

I wasn't sure I believed her, but it was her lunch. When it was my turn to pick, we were going to Tujague's for gumbo.

"I think I might have found a house you could decorate for the home tour," I said after the server set a basket of old school crudité on the table. Not as good as breadsticks but not bad. "Nothing definite but I've got a lead."

Even that might be overstating things. I still had no idea how I was going to get Jensen to agree to open his home but seeing the expression on my friend's face made me determined to figure it out.

"How? Who? They always show the same houses. They're locked up years in advance."

"I know someone with a house in the Garden District that's never been featured." Knew—intimately, like screaming orgasm, fist gripping my hair, just shy of Biblical depending on how you counted it—someone who had a home that had never been shown. "I'm…" *How did I describe it? Close to? Seeing? Cuffed by?* It *wasn't* dating. "I have a client who has a home on First Street. I might be able to convince him to open it up."

Holding a forkful of spiralized zucchini halfway to her mouth, she looked at me like I'd offered her the Holy Grail. "On First? Whose house is it? I thought you weren't seeing clients."

Elena was my friend. It ought to be easier to tell her the truth about Erik and me.

"Remember the speaker from the domestic violence fundraiser?"

"Erik Jensen is your client?" Her voice rose on his name, reaching near screech levels, and I wondered if somewhere across town, the good counselor's ears were ringing.

"Shh," I said, holding my hands up between us.

"Sorry." She dropped her voice in a mock whisper. "But seriously? Since when do you know Erik Jensen? Why didn't you say something about it at the benefit?

Have you seen him naked? God, I can't believe you've been holding out on me."

It wasn't lost on me that she'd started speaking almost entirely in questions. Questions I wasn't comfortable answering—not yet anyway.

"I didn't know him at the benefit," I said, opting for the easiest answer.

"But you know him now? Even though you aren't seeing any new clients because of the legal thing?"

This time her questions came with a side of accusation and I felt like an ass. *So much for the new, more honest Alex.*

"It's complicated."

"I bet it is." She pinned me with her stare and I watched as her eyes went wide. "You're dating Erik Jensen. That's it, isn't it? He's one of the most eligible bachelors in the city. He's almost never seen with the same woman more than once. There'd been speculation that he was gay. You'd be Amal to his Clooney."

Something inside my chest tightened, both at the idea of having to disabuse her of her Amal Clooney dreams and more shocking, at the fact that some of those kind of dreams seemed to have crept into my head as well. That wouldn't do. Erik and I were playing *tie me up/tie me down*, not playing house. I chose to ignore for the moment that his house was exactly what I'd be asking him for.

"Slow down. It's not like that. We're not dating. We're friends." I pulled the word out of the air at the last minute, but when I rolled it around in my head, I realized I liked the way it felt.

I could do a hell of a lot worse than have a friend like Erik. He was an arrogant, infuriating know-it-all, but he was also attentive, perceptive, challenging, and maybe most surprisingly, kind.

"Friends with benefits or just friends?"

"We're friends." I left everything else unsaid. If I talked out my feelings with Elena, I wouldn't be able to hide them from myself, and it felt like my peace of mind depended on it.

"Do you really think he'd be willing to do it?" she asked, looking like a woman who didn't want to be disappointed.

Welcome to the club, sister.

I WAITED UNTIL I got back to my apartment before I called Erik. Not bothering with something as mundane as a plate, I took a bite of the waxed paper-wrapped muffaletta sandwich, thumbed open the contact for Sir and hit Call. I groaned in satisfaction as the salty olive salad and salami soothed my squash-abused taste buds.

"Mid-orgasm, kitten, or just getting started?" he answered and I realized he must have heard my cured Italian meat-induced pleasure.

"Eating. It's a long story."

"I'm happy to make time for you."

My stomach warmed both from the food and his words. I could picture him standing in his office, sleeves rolled up to reveal his tanned wrists while he surveyed everything around him like the lord of his domain. I didn't want to talk about my foray into raw food. Everything we'd done together had this undercurrent of delicious sensuality. It might break my heart if denial was something he actually enjoyed.

"I have a question."

"I have many answers," he said, the smile clear in his voice.

"Are we friends?"

He paused for a moment and I wondered if he was worried it was some kind of trick question. Or worse if, because I'd accidentally dropped the *L* bomb, he was trying to find a nice way to tell me no. The possibility made me freeze in place, and I opened my mouth to tell him never mind. I didn't want to know.

"Yes, Alexandra, I believe we are friends." He let out a hmpf on the other end of the line, and I got the impression the answer surprised him as much as it initially surprised me. "Why did you ask?"

"I need a favor."

"You want me to strap a vibrator to your clit, bend you over the spanking bench and warm your ass with my hand until you come three or four times?"

My skin flushed at his words. It wasn't fair that he could make my body respond like that, to nothing more than the sound of his voice and the picture he painted with his words. I shifted on my ladies who lunch heels, pressing my thighs together to keep from trying to crawl through the phone to curl up on his lap, begging to be stroked like the kitten he called me.

"I want you to let me enter your house in the Garden District Home Tour. I can't tell you why—at least not now—but it's important. And you won't have to do a thing." I cringed, waiting for the *no* I knew was coming.

"Get your sweet ass ready, and I'll have the car pick you up in an hour. Wear that naughty librarian skirt, the highest heels you have and no panties. We'll try my favor first while I consider yours."

I sagged against the counter, using it to steady my shaky legs. "Yes, Sir," I said, before I could stop myself, the title a response to the command in his voice.

"See you in an hour, friend." He disconnected the call, his warm chuckle still ringing in my ear.

ERIK

"COUNT THEM OUT for me, beautiful."

Alex was stretched over the spanking bench in my playroom, her skirt rucked up around her waist, her naked ass in the air just waiting for my hand. Every time she shifted on her stilettos, I got a fucking spectacular glimpse of the lips of her pretty pink pussy.

"Yes, Sir." She glanced over her shoulder and her expression made it clear she was feeling more smart ass than submissive.

Not that the two were mutually exclusive, but we were both going to have a lot more fun if I could get her out of her head. I ran my hand over the smooth, round globe of her ass. *The woman had a fine ass.* Instead of tensing, she pushed back into my palm, moving toward the caress. I pulled my hand back and smacked her hard. Hard enough to make my palm sting and for her to jump like a scalded cat.

"Fucking hell, Jensen. That hurt." She glared over her shoulder at me, her eyes burning.

"And we're going to have to do it again because you didn't count it out." I pitched my voice low and kept my tone reasonable, as if I were reciting a legal brief. I knew the lack of emotion would wind her even higher and the faster she surrendered, the better for both of us. Although I'd be happy to play with her for as long as she let me.

"The hell we are." She pushed her chest off the bench. I hadn't bound her this time because I wanted to see if she could stay still. Apparently, she couldn't.

"Are you using your safe word, Alexandra?"

She looked like she'd happily shoot daggers out of her eyes at me if she could, but she shook her head.

"I need to hear you say it."

"No, I'm not using my safe word."

I could have sworn she muttered something under her breath that sounded a lot like *you ass*, but we were still taking baby steps so I pretended not to hear.

"Good. Count."

I watched her body tense. The muscles of her butt tightened as she braced herself. I raised my hand but instead of spanking her, I fiddled with the remote in my pocket, turning on the tiny vibe pressed against her clit. Her breath went out in a rush and she rocked back on her heels, moving toward the sensation. That's when I struck, a stinging smack across her ass, not as hard as the first time but hard enough to leave a red handprint on her pale skin.

"One." She gritted the words out between clenched teeth.

"That's it, kitten. I almost thought you'd forgotten again." I didn't bother to try to hide my grin.

She didn't comment on the pet name, which meant she was too busy trying to hold herself together to pay any attention to me beyond what my hand would do next. I liked messing with her—ruffling her carefully controlled world—but I fucking loved being the one who got to tip her over the edge. I bumped up the intensity with the remote in my pocket and brought my hand down on her tender skin again, softer but in the same place as before. She squeaked out the word *two* as she squirmed on the pencil-thin points of her heels. There was no way for her to get any relief from the vibrator on her clit or my hand on her ass. Not unless she was willing to use her safe word and we both knew she'd never do that. It would take a lot more than a simple spanking to get her to give up.

I didn't want her to give up. I wanted her to give in. I ran my hand over her ass, feeling the heat of her flushed skin against my palm. When I trailed my fingers between her legs, dipping into her slick folds, she rocked back into my touch, angling her hips to get closer to my fingers. Trying to steer instead of going along for the ride.

I pulled my hand away and turned off the vibe. She let out a frustrated cry but rather than waiting to see if she'd say anything, I brought my palm down on her other cheek. Hard. My hand made a satisfying red print on her ass and she yelped out *three* as her body tensed in anticipation.

I turned the vibe up to full power and slapped her ass twice in quick succession, one stinging blow right on top of the other.

"Did you forget something, beautiful?"

"Four. Five. God." She panted the words out and I could see the last of her careful control starting to fray.

"Just in time. I was afraid we'd have to start over again."

She let out a whimper, and I hit a button on the remote that turned the vibe to an intermittent pulse. It had a pattern but it was long enough between repeats that she'd have a hard time anticipating the sensation.

"Please, Erik. Please."

"Please what, sweetheart?"

Her skin flushed a pretty rose not just from my hands, but from her desire, and her breath came in shallow gasps. I could see the slick arousal on her pussy and it took every bit of control I possessed to keep from pulling out my cock and sinking balls-deep inside her, driving into her with long, punishing strokes of my aching cock until we both got what we needed. When we were finished with this bit of play, I was going to have a long talk with myself and try to remember why I wasn't having sex with Alex. At the moment, I had no fucking idea.

"Please make me come."

I flipped the vibe back to full power and brought my hand down in rapid slaps, not hard but too fast for her to catch her bearings.

"Six. Seven. Eight. Oooh." Her back arched, pressing her ass in the air like some kind of fucking erotic offering, and her legs started to shake.

I slid my hand between her legs, teasing her opening with the tip of my finger. It reminded me of the old *just the tip* joke, but my throat was too tight from wanting her to laugh at anything.

"You are so wet for me. So beautiful. God, Alex."

I felt my control start to slip. Plunging my fingers inside her, I pressed forward, curving until I felt the spongy place I was looking for. Stroking in and out of her with one hand, I brought my other hand down hard on the fleshy part of her ass.

"Count, Alex." It was my turn to grit my teeth. My turn to hold onto the last vestiges of my control.

"Nine." She sobbed the word. "Coming. Erik. Fuck, I'm coming."

I smacked her one last time as I felt her body clench around me, pulsing as her tight cunt milked my fingers. Hitting the button on the remote, I turned off the vibe and rubbed gentle circles on her abused ass as the last of the climax rolled through her. Gazing down at the woman drawing shaky breaths in front of me, the gorgeous, incredibly strong woman who'd given herself to me, I felt something in my chest tighten. *If she was the one submitting, why did it feel like I was the one being mastered?*

Alex

THE AIRY INSTRUMENTAL MUSIC ENDED
and the yoga instructor slowly turned the lights on around
the perimeter of the room. If I could figure out a way to
just show up for the last fifteen minutes of class and the
guided meditation while I sacked out on my mat, I'd go to
yoga every day. Twice a day.

I actually hadn't minded the poses this time. Even
the core sequence felt good for a change, instead of like
slow torture. After my time with Erik, my whole body felt
alive, as if even in the absence of his touch, my skin was
somehow more sensitive. I could get used to the feeling
but I still wasn't sure how I felt about the spanking. Or
rather, I was sure I loved it—like came so hard I saw stars
and might have screamed myself hoarse—but I wasn't
sure how I felt about loving it. If I got off on the naughty
schoolgirl thing, on the equivalent of Erik turning me over
his knee and *punishing* me, what did it mean? I had a lot of
feelings to work through on the issue, but I knew without
a doubt I'd bend over for him again if he asked me.

The only part that felt off was the lack of sex,
which was maybe not accurate considering the multiple
orgasms and the amount of time I'd spent naked with him.

It didn't matter; it wasn't the same. I wanted him inside me, moving above me or under me. I didn't care about the specifics. I wanted to feel myself joined to him, not just through mutual pleasure, a real *I take your body into mine* kind of union. It was as if he'd uncovered an empty space inside me only he could fill, and every time we were together, the ache got stronger.

I understood why he'd insisted on no sex in the beginning. It really cheesed my biscuits that he'd been the emotionally mature one of us, but he'd been right. I was so used to using sex for power even when I wasn't having it. I never would have surrendered and made myself vulnerable if he hadn't held the line. And that meant I'd never have felt all the things I was feeling with him. I was ready to go farther. I'd been sure he was too and then at the last minute, he pulled back and pulled away.

"Ready to go?" asked Meredith, waving her hand in front of me. "You zoned out on me for a minute there." She'd already rolled up her mat and stood in front of me, hand on her hip, looking like some kind of Celtic goddess. It didn't matter how hard the class was; she never looked like she'd been working.

"Yeah. Sorry," I said, shaking myself back to the present. I rolled up my mat and shoved my feet into my shoes before falling into step beside her.

"Want to go to Mocha & Mine? They've got those chili ganache things you like this week."

We had a standing arrangement. I did yoga with her because I had to do some kind of exercise and I hated yoga the least, and she went with me for coffee and chocolate afterward. Or pralines. I could be flexible with the treat as long as our calorie intake came close to meeting our expenditure.

"Sounds good." I glanced over and caught her watching me, her green eyes intent. "What?"

"I'm not sure," she said, searching my face. "There's something different with you. There wasn't nearly as much bitching as usual and you seem lighter. I don't know—different somehow. The last time we got together, you were popping antacids like they were M&M's. What changed? Did Charlotte get the lawsuit dropped?"

My steps faltered at the mention of the lawsuit. I'd been so wrapped up in Erik—tied up by Erik—I hadn't asked Charlotte about the status of the suit against my company. I knew she'd tell me if something big came up but it bugged me that I'd so quickly re-ordered my priorities around a man. It bothered me more that when I thought about going back to work, my chest tightened in an uncomfortable way. My bills were paid up for the month and I had a little bit of money in my checking account and a couple of months' worth of expenses in my money market, but unless something changed with the lawsuit, and quick, I was going to have to figure out another way to support myself.

"Nope. No change." I left it there. The rest of my feelings were too complicated to talk about before a serious infusion of cacao.

"It's something."

I didn't offer an explanation. I wasn't ready to talk about Erik, not until I had a better understanding of how I felt about things and what the hell—besides the obvious bondage stuff—we were doing. After another half block, she stopped guessing and turned her attention back to the street in front of us. The coffee shop was four blocks from the yoga studio and this time of day, the streets were clogged with tourists and traffic.

I'd sweated through my T-shirt again by the time the door of the café closed on the heat outside, trapping us in coffee-scented air-conditioned bliss. We placed our coffee orders and got a pound of assorted chocolate truffles to share, heavy on the chili ones I loved. While I waited for the barista to call my name, I scanned the small tins lining the side wall. I'd never really paid attention before but they had lavender-infused Earl Grey in a pretty gray-purple tin and a dozen or so other choices. Nowhere near as many as in the tea shop Erik and I visited, but there was a black tea with orange peel that looked interesting and a lapsang with ginger I wanted to see if Erik liked. I picked up three of the tins and headed to register.

"Tea?" asked Meredith. "I thought you only drank coffee." She pinned me with her too-perceptive gaze, and I tried to figure out how to explain that they weren't for me without mentioning that they were for someone else.

"I drink tea sometimes."

"No. You don't. You drink coffee by the industrial carafe size. I've never seen you drink tea."

"It's a new thing. I've got a friend who got me into it." I shrugged as if it were the most natural explanation in the world.

"Oh my God, you've met someone. You're in love." She let out a squeal so loud it was a miracle the plate glass window stayed intact.

"Ow." I juggled the tins so I could stick my finger in my ear to stop the ringing. I don't know why people do that. It didn't help. "Maybe dial it back a couple hundred decibels, and no, I'm not in love." *I wasn't, was I?* I mean, there was the tea but that's what friends did—get things for each other. Erik and I had already established we were friends. More disturbing were the re-ordered priorities, but that didn't mean I was in love. *Did it? Fuck.*

Meredith grabbed my elbow, dragged me to the counter to pay for the tea and hurried me to a table in the back of the restaurant before releasing me.

"My coffee," I said, looking plaintively at the counter. It felt like I was miles from caffeine and cacao faced with nothing but a ginger in her full power, determined to help me sort through my feelings.

"Relax, you big baby," she said, sounding uncharacteristically demanding. Meredith was usually the nice one. "I'll get your coffee after you tell me his name. And don't bother trying to deny it."

"It's complicated," I said, trying to work out how to tell her about Erik without telling her everything about him.

And then reconsidered before I opened my mouth because, as it turned out, I actually wanted someone to talk to about him who wasn't obsessed with attorney-client privilege. I loved Charlotte and I knew she loved me, but given the way we started, I wasn't sure she'd ever be able to see him through anything other than her lawyer filter. We were way beyond that. Hell, I wasn't sure that's where we'd even started. I'd have to check with him, but I'd bet we'd both built a pretty extensive fantasy around each other before we got to the deposition. I know I had. I hadn't been ready to tell Elena. I was ready now.

"His name's Erik. And I'm not in love. At least I don't think I am."

Managing to stifle another squeal, Meredith hugged me while I collapsed back into my chair, wondering how I'd ever let things get this far. Erik and I were supposed to be playing at Bondage 101. Hell, maybe 501. He could teach a graduate-level course on floggers alone. We'd crossed over from adversaries to friends, but honestly, that was supposed to be it. Emotions had no place in anything we'd done.

Except they did. I'd been more honest with Erik than I'd been with any other man. Maybe because we'd started out not needing to impress each other, maybe because he demanded honesty in my responses to him, and we were both too damn competitive to cheat or give up. I thought back to the way he'd cradled me in his arms as I read to him. The way he said *he* needed to hold me. He'd been the one doing the spanking, but I hadn't been the only one making myself vulnerable.

Did that mean he'd let his emotions get involved too? A freaking colony of butterflies set up residence in my stomach and the whiplash pulled me up short. I wanted him involved—emotionally invested up to his eyeballs— and I didn't want to ever talk to him about any of it. In equal measures. Trying to hold two thoughts that couldn't exist simultaneously threatened to strip the last bit of my control.

"Hold on a minute," said Meredith, her forehead creased in concern. "I'll go get your coffee and then we'll talk."

I nodded, not sure I could manage more without caffeine. I glanced down at the bag holding the tea canisters still clutched in my arms and fought the visceral urge to fling them away. Like maybe if I ignored my feelings for Erik, they might disappear. I opted for setting the bag on the floor beside me and stared at my empty hands resting on the café tabletop until Meredith came back with my macchiato and a small box of truffles. She set the cup in my hands and opened the box, revealing the balls of chocolatey goodness.

"Let's start with the easy question. Where did you meet this Erik?" She took a swallow of her coffee and waited, watching me, presumably for signs I planned to bolt and take the truffles with me.

I popped one in my mouth instead and waited for the rich chocolate with its slight hit of cayenne to hit my system, washing it down with the rich frothy coffee.

"He was the attorney behind the cease-and-desist motion."

"No shit?" Meredith's green eyes went wide and she blew out a breath. "No wonder you don't look happy about the love thing. How did you manage this?"

"He hired me." I popped another truffle—hazelnut this time—in my mouth and told her everything. When I got to the flogger and *Outlander*, she made me wait until she refilled our macchiatos, calories be damned. By the time we got to the part where I admitted I'd fallen in love with the arrogant attorney, the truffles were long gone, and I was feeling a sense of loss that had nothing to do with the lack of chocolate.

I'd made a rookie mistake and confused good—fuck, phenomenal—sex with intimacy. I'd fallen in love with a man who wasn't looking for a relationship. Hell, in the beginning, he hadn't been looking for anything other than to teach me a lesson. I ignored the fact that I'd learned that lesson and more and pushed aside all the other things we'd done together. The sweet things. The things I knew I'd miss when we walked away. There was no reason to compound the mistake I'd already made by going farther down a road I was sure led to a dead end.

ERIK

I SCANNED THE page for the fifth time, still losing the thread of the words before I reached the end. I was used to dealing with the challenge reading presented me. I had a half dozen coping mechanisms and worked them like a boss. Most of the time it didn't matter, but when I was distracted, all bets were off. It seemed like since I met Alex, I was always distracted.

I had one more brief to finish before I could leave for the weekend. I'd cleared my schedule and told my assistant I was unavailable to anyone—including paralegals and clients—unless there was actual bloodshed involved. Anything short of incarceration could wait until Monday. I wanted two uninterrupted days with Alex, and I was willing to move heaven and earth to get them.

I gave up on trying to read the words in front of me and put in my earbud instead, activating the text-to-speech app to read the file to me. Even that reminded me of her and the photo she'd sent me during my meeting. The way she'd looked stretched out in the tub.

"Enough," I muttered to myself and blew out a breath. I'd listen to the brief in the car. Anything else could wait. "I'm gone for the weekend." Not bothering to wait for a response, I strode past my assistant's desk, not breaking stride until I reached the bank of elevators.

"Where are you going in such a hurry?" Jared fell into step beside me.

"Away." I didn't want to explain things to anyone. I wanted to pick up Alex, take her home and fuck her senseless.

I'd come to a realization the last time we were together. The not having sex thing was completely arbitrary. I'd touched every inch of her and she'd had her mouth all over me. I fucking loved the way she sucked cock—like I was her new favorite toy—but I wanted more. We were friends, clearly with benefits, and I intended to start benefiting. Over and over until we were too exhausted to move. Maybe then I'd be able to concentrate on something other than the woman who'd invaded every corner of my head. Alex had me twisted in knots, as evidenced by the fact that I'd even considered having my house included on the home tour. *Who knew what the hell would be next if I didn't get a grip on myself?*

"I gathered that, asshole."

He waited a moment, clearly assuming I'd offer more details. He'd be waiting a long damn time. I punched the elevator button again, willing it to hurry up

"Jackson says they're close to settling the Gentleman's Submissive case. As soon as the paperwork's filed, he'll cancel the cease-and-desist. The client never really had the stomach to go to trial."

Of course they hadn't. I'd been the one pushing to go to trial. Back when I'd wanted to ruin Alex instead of tuck her into my bed. I raised my finger to punch the damn button again when the ramifications of what Jared said hit me. Without the cease-and-desist, Alex would be free to take on other clients again. Nothing about that worked for me. Not that I had any say in it. We weren't exclusive.

Hell, we were barely in a relationship. *Fuck me*. I wanted both of those things.

Not the two kids, white picket fences and happily ever after. I was never going down that path, but Alex as my full-time submissive? Hell yeah, I wanted that. She'd want it too when she saw the upside. I went into full denial about my chances to convince Alex to give up on the business she'd built. I shouldn't even want that. Friends wanted the best for each other. I'd just have to figure out a new best—one that had her naked, under my hands and mouth as often as possible and away from all other men. Piece of cake. *Fuck me.*

"So where are you really going?"

I glanced over, surprised to still find Jared standing next to me. The door opened and I stepped inside the car.

"I'm spending the weekend with Alex," I said as the elevator closed on his shit-eating grin.

I made it across town in record time and double-parked because I didn't want to take the extra time to get to her. She must have felt some of the same urgency as me. I made it as far as the front door to her building when she came down the stairs. Looking like every fantasy I'd ever had come to life. Black stilettos, black pencil-thin skirt, crisp white menswear-styled shirt that made me picture her in my house wearing nothing but my dress shirt, and red lacquered lips I couldn't wait to have wrapped around my cock. I was hard just thinking about it.

"Hello, beautiful." I took her by the elbow and leaned in to nuzzle her neck, breathing in the rich scent of peonies and roses.

"Hey you." She tipped her head, offering me the long, slender column of her neck, and gripped the lapels of my suit coat.

One of us needed to move and quick, or I was going to push her up against the wall, sink my hands into her sleek hair and set about smearing her lipstick.

"Are you sure I don't need to bring anything for the weekend? You haven't told me what we're doing."

I'd thought about taking her somewhere exotic, but as soon as I decided to abandon my no-sex plan, all I could think about was getting inside her as quickly as possible. Travel time didn't figure into that. My house, with its playroom and collection of toys, felt too far away, but if I hit the lights right, we could be pulling into my drive in fifteen minutes.

"I have everything you need," I said, arching an eyebrow at her.

She rolled her eyes but I could see the way her pulse kicked up at her throat. She wanted this too. *Now to convince her to go along with the rest of my idea.*

Alex

I WAS NERVOUS. WHAT KIND of sense did that make? I'd been naked and tied up with this man, on my knees with his cock down my throat. He had given me handfuls of orgasms. It wasn't like it was our first date or something. We *knew* each other. I don't know if it was my talk with Meredith and dragging my emotions out into the clear light of day or if it was because he'd agreed to open his house on the home tour for me. Something I knew he didn't want to do. Something he'd done because he at least had some kind of feelings for me beyond the tie me up/tie me down kind. Regardless of the reason, something had changed.

He didn't touch me on the ride to his house. His hands stayed at ten and two and his gaze straight ahead, as if he was demanding the distance to close between us and our destination by sheer force of will. He pulled the car into the circle behind the house and was out his door and around to my side of the car before I managed to get free of my seat belt. Instead of offering me his hand or some other kind of civilized response, he hoisted me up into his arms, planting his shoulder in my mid-section in a kind of fireman's carry.

"Neanderthal!" I gasped out between giggles.

"And proud of it."

He smacked my ass hard enough to make me yelp and then we were through the door and up the stairs to his bedroom, and I lost my breath for a completely different reason. I'd gotten a quick glimpse of the room on our previous tour, but I'd never been inside. We played in the playroom or in his sitting room. We'd never done anything as mundane as get in bed together, but there it was, standing like the down pillow duvet-covered equivalent of a flashing neon sign.

Erik set me on my feet just long enough to cradle my face in his hands and kiss me like I was the air he needed to breathe and then his fingers went to work on my shirt. He wrestled with the tiny buttons, his fingers uncharacteristically clumsy.

"Take it off," he said, his voice strained in a way that sent heat curling low in my body. "All of it. I want every single scrap of clothing between your skin and my mouth off. Now."

I made quick work of the buttons while he yanked on his tie, freeing it from his collar with a snap that made my mouth water. He undid two buttons and then grabbed the open collar of his shirt and hauled it over his head. I paused in the middle of toeing off my shoes to drink in his spectacular chest. Seriously, there were valleys and ridges etched across the planes of his stomach, and I planned to follow every single one. With my tongue.

"Move, Alex," he said, reaching for his belt.

I slid off my heels and made quick work of my blouse and skirt. I'd worn white lace panties and a sheer white demi bra because he seemed to like the naughty librarian thing. I'd smoothed my hair into a French twist for the same reason. At the moment, he didn't look like he was interested in anything other than devouring me. He pinned me with his gaze as I stripped off the lace, baring myself completely. The naked hunger in his eyes made my mouth water and I took a step closer and reached for his waistband.

"Not this time." He twisted out of my grasp. "On the bed, beautiful, back against the pillows, knees up and legs spread wide. Hold onto the headboard and don't let go until I tell you or I'll bind you in place so you can't get away from me."

The implied threat added an edge to my desire and for a fraction of a second, I debated defying him to see what would happen. Then he pushed his pants over his hips, revealing his hard cock stretching out from under the waistband of his boxer briefs, and my focus narrowed to finding the fastest way to get him in bed with me. To take him inside me.

Unwilling to look away for even a moment, I scooted up the bed until my back hit the wall of pillows. Keeping my gaze pinned to the gorgeous half-naked man in front of me, I reached over my head and grabbed the metal bar on the headboard. The position pushed my breasts forward but he kept his attention on my face while he stripped off the last of his clothing. His hard, thick cock jutted in front of him and I licked my lips—not from some artificial attempt at seducing him—because I couldn't wait to take him in my mouth and suck him until his head fell back and the muscles of his neck tensed as he came apart under my tongue.

"Fuck, Alex. The way you're looking at me." He shook his head as he stalked toward me. "Spread your legs for me, sweetheart. The sooner I make you come, the sooner I can give both of us what we want."

Bending my knees, I hurried to comply. I planted the heels of my feet in the soft duvet and opened my legs, letting him see every inch of me, exposing every bit of my already soaked sex.

"That's it, beautiful. You are so fucking wet. Just for me. For me to taste. For me to fuck."

Erik crawled onto the bed and my stomach tightened in anticipation. We'd done plenty of things to each other. I'd had lots and lots of orgasms with this man, but we'd never been together like this. Both of us naked. The filthy, possessive words pushed every one of my boundaries and made me want to give everything to this man who'd somehow made me feel so much.

"I'm close," I said, my voice a breathy whisper. "I'm already so close. Fuck me, please."

His answering growl stripped the last of my control and reduced me to begging.

"Please, Erik. I need you to fuck me. Please."

He moved up my body and for a moment, I thought he'd relent and give me what I knew we both wanted. Instead, he kissed me, cupping my head and working my hair free from its pins.

"Not yet. I want you so much it hurts but when I finally sink into your tight little pussy, I'm not going to be able to stop myself, so you have to come first."

He nipped at my earlobe and I tipped my head, baring my throat to him like an animal for her mate. For the first time in my life, I realized what it meant to hand that kind of control to someone else. The idea rocked me to my core, but I didn't doubt for a second that Erik was man enough to handle it, to trust with everything.

"Don't distract me or we're going to have to start all over again." He scraped his teeth gently over the pulse point at the base of my throat and then worked his way down my body until he was wedged between my thighs.

Palming my ass, he kissed me, sucking on my clit and tracing my labia with the flat of his tongue. I white-knuckled the headboard, desperate to hold on, to stay still so he had no reason to make good on his threat. I was already so close just from imagining this moment. It wouldn't take anything to push me over the edge. Pressing his thumb against my opening, he wrapped his lips around my clit and sucked, hard rhythmic pulses that pushed me higher and higher, desire coiling tight deep inside until there was nowhere else for it to go. No way to hold it inside me.

"Erik. Fuck. God, I'm coming."

He kept up the delicious, relentless onslaught with his mouth until my legs shook and I was squirming to get a break to catch my breath.

"Please," I said, tears leaking from the corners of my eyes. "I need …"

"I know, baby." He pressed his lips to the inside of my thigh before sucking on the tender skin. Knowing I'd wear his mark gave me a perverse amount of pleasure. Even if he and I were the only ones who knew. I didn't want to think about what that meant. I didn't want to think about my feelings or anything beyond finally taking Erik inside me.

Getting to his knees, he reached for a condom on the nightstand, and I watched, spellbound, as he sheathed himself. Nothing mattered but the two of us. The world didn't exist beyond the boundary of Erik's bed.

"I've wanted this for so damn long," he said, gripping my hips and positioning himself at my opening. "Since the moment you fell into my arms."

"Me, too." I pulled against the headboard, raising myself up as far as I could so I could watch him enter me.

I was slick and swollen, and he fought for every inch, stretching me, giving me a chance to get used to the delicious invasion before sinking the whole way home. I felt the slap of his balls against my ass and then he froze, fingers tight on my hips, holding completely still. The muscles on his neck corded and his stomach tightened as if he were fighting a battle with himself.

"You feel so fucking good, sweetheart. So fucking good."

And then he started to move and there wasn't space for words. There wasn't room for anything but the way our bodies wedded together. He bent over me, claiming my lips as he drove inside me, fucking my mouth with his tongue as his cock filled me. I gave up trying to be still, gave up holding onto the headboard and twined my arms around his neck, tugging his hair to pull him closer.

Cradling my head to his chest, he sat up, taking me with him until I straddled his lap, his cock hitting so deep inside me, I felt him everywhere.

"Take what you need, beautiful. Come for me again." Gripping my hand, he guided our fingers to my aching clit. I rode our combined hands and his cock as he drove himself up into me, pushing us higher with each thrust. Pleasure spiraled in on itself, filling me until I couldn't hold it any longer.

"Coming. God, I'm coming." I gasped out the words as the climax rocketed through me, tightening everything before releasing me to shatter into a million beautiful pieces.

Erik clutched me to him, gripping my hip and cradling my head as he drove up into me with an uncontrolled passion. I clung to him, sobbing his name as he came apart in my arms.

ERIK

I WOKE WITH Alex in my arms and too many questions working their way around in my brain to let me sleep. I hadn't slept with a woman since Julie and not really anyone before that. There was an intimacy in sleep, a vulnerability. I'd never really cared for it before. I'd done it in other relationships because it was the next logical step and the woman expected it but it had been a compromise. Something I did for them, not because I wanted it myself. I fucking loved waking with Alex curled against me, her warm body fitted to mine as if we were two pieces of a puzzle finally joined together. I wanted to sleep that way every night.

Clearly, I'd lost my mind. Dr. Smithson and I—it felt so long since I'd thought of her like that—were exploring the finer points of BDSM and pushing the boundaries to include recreational fucking. We weren't in a relationship. At least we weren't supposed to be. We'd never negotiated for that, which didn't mean I couldn't fix it. I might not be able to offer her a house full of children and porch rockers but that didn't mean we couldn't come to some kind of mutually beneficial relationship.

If Jared was right, Alex would be able to go back to seeing clients in a matter of days. My grip tightened reflexively on her hip and I forced my hand to relax before I woke her. I intended to do that by sliding my cock inside her as soon as I got my head in the right place. We'd covered a lot of ground before we fell asleep but there were still dozens of things I wanted to do with her and that was just off the top of my head. I hadn't begun to dig deep.

I hated the idea of her being with anyone else, another first for me. Jealousy never usually played into my feelings. If she didn't see clients, she'd need something else to do. It wasn't like I could call in some favors and hook her up with a gender studies professorship. I ran through the list of people I knew in academics just to make sure but no—no magic job there. If there were jobs to be had, she wouldn't need my help anyway. We might have disagreements on what it meant to be dominant and submissive, but I didn't have any doubt Alex was more than capable of making her own way. I was as crazy about her brilliant mind as I was about her body.

I seriously doubted I could get her to take up law, so paralegal was out. Which meant she'd go back to her business, and I'd go back to being screwed. Unless I figured out a way to blend the two together.

She'd let me pay her for sessions before. What if I became her only client—not forever; neither one of us fit the courtesan-benefactor stereotype—just in the short-term until we figured out what we were doing together. Maybe another month or two and we'd be out of each other's systems and on to whatever came next. The thought felt off, disingenuous. Wrong. Holding Alex's sleeping warmth in my arms, I had a hard time imagining ever being willing to say good-bye. I didn't have to figure any of that out now. Being her only client would let me kick the can down the road for a bit. Maybe by the time I ran out of asphalt, I'd have another, better plan in place. *Maybe.*

Alex let out a soft snore and I grinned into the early dawn light. Things like that weren't supposed to be sexy, but everything about this woman in my arms made me want her a little more. I curled around her, rolling her on her side so I could fit my cock against the soft seam of her ass. She rocked back in her sleep, wedging tighter into me. My chest tightened, knowing she wanted me, that she'd move toward me, even in sleep. Pressing my lips to the back of her neck, I breathed in sex, warm woman and the rich floral scent she wore. I slid my hand from her hip over the gentle swell of her stomach to cup her breast.

For a moment, I just lay there holding a sleeping Alex in my arms, a sense of certainty that things were exactly the way they were supposed to be washing over me. I didn't know what it meant or how I planned to reorder my life to include her. I hadn't planned on a relationship, but I wasn't ready to let the lifting of the lawsuit create an artificial deadline and I sure as hell wasn't ready to share. I squeezed her breast possessively.

"Everything okay?" she said, her voice a sleepy murmur.

"Better than okay."

Spreading her thighs wide enough to allow me to position my cock against her slick opening, I teased her clit with my fingers, urging her body's response. In one smooth motion, I thrust inside her, losing myself in the overwhelming sensation of having her skin to skin, no barriers between us. Curled around her, holding her in my arms, I started to move.

"THE MAN CAN work a flogger and a spatula." I sat at Erik's kitchen island, wearing nothing but a threadbare Tulane University T-shirt that smelled like him. He'd woken me with an orgasm and the promise of breakfast and he'd delivered on both. Dude was some kind of sex god who handled an omelet almost as deftly as he handled my clit.

"What can I say; I aim to please." He arched an eyebrow in false modesty before polishing off the last of his eggs.

He'd slipped an apron over his bare chest while he made breakfast, which made sense from an unwanted burn standpoint but was a sad waste of spectacular abs. Now that I'd seen all of the man's body—run my tongue over it—I had a hard time with even the concept of clothing. It was like putting a drape over Michelangelo's *David*. Some things should never be covered. Of course, that would mean no suits or ties. I licked the cheese off the back of my fork, weighing the pros and cons in my head.

"You keep looking at me like that, kitten, and I'm going to bend you over the kitchen counter and fuck you again before you finish your breakfast."

"We're back to kitten. I thought we'd moved past that," I said, trying to sound incensed but failing because too much of my cognitive power was tied up in finding a flaw in the countertop plan. The eggs were good, exceptional even, but still just eggs. I could eat any time.

His expression shifted and for a moment, instead of sexy pirate, he looked like he was trying to puzzle something out. It was an unusual glimpse of uncertainty from a man normally confident to a fault.

"We've definitely moved past where we started." His gaze searched my face and I froze in place, my forkful of cheesy eggs momentarily forgotten.

To say that things between us had changed was an understatement. At the deposition, he hated me. Now we were at least friends and lovers in the literal sense. I muffled the part of me that hoped we were more, the part of my psyche that had wandered unprotected down the path toward the *L* word. Knowing it was true and saying the whole word even in my head were two completely different things.

"One of the partners at my firm told me they're almost ready to settle your case. Which means the cease-and-desist will be removed."

The fork clattered to my plate. I'd known the suit was moving forward. Charlotte had told me as much, but I hadn't realized we were so close to the end.

"How soon?" I had so many thoughts and emotions rolling around in my head. The cease-and-desist had given us a kind of pocket of space to explore this thing between us. Its removal presented an arbitrary deadline. One I didn't yet understand.

"A couple of days, which got me thinking." He stood, closing the distance between us, spinning my stool around to face him. "I don't want you to see anyone else." He gripped my hips, fitting himself between my legs and making me way too aware of my naked sex. "I want it to just be you and me."

The breath caught in my throat at the possibility that we might actually be feeling the same thing. That this thing between us might stop being a thing and start being the relationship I hadn't let myself believe I wanted. It would make work a challenge. I didn't know how I'd deal with it, but we could figure it out—set boundaries, sort through expectations, that kind of thing. I was willing to compromise to make things work. The love-wielding part of my psyche started dancing her way out of the closet I'd shoved her into.

"I was thinking I could pay you to be your only client. Not long-term, of course. Just until we got each other out of our systems. I'm not a relationship person, and I don't think you are either, but I'm not finished with you yet. I want more time."

He searched my face, waiting for my response as the meaning of his words finally penetrated my thick head. *He wasn't falling in love. He wasn't falling in anything.* He just wanted to fuck awhile longer, and he didn't like to share. All perfectly reasonable things considering where we'd started. And he was willing to pay for the privilege of getting what he wanted.

This man I loved—no sense lying about it now—who didn't love me, this man who could own me body and soul with his touch, wanted to *buy* me.

I felt my heart start to fracture and reorder itself to this new kind of normal, and then I gave him the only answer I could.

"Mercy."

ERIK

"YOU'RE IN EARLY," SAID JARED, leaning against the doorframe to my office. "I didn't expect you to come rolling in here until after nine, looking all rested and refreshed from your weekend sex-a-thon." He crossed the office and dropped into one of the leather client chairs, pinning me with his prosecutor's gaze. "You look like shit. What happened? Tell me you didn't fuck things up with the doctor lady."

"Fuck off." I didn't want to talk about Alex. Hell, I didn't want to think about Alex, not that it had done me any good. I hadn't been able to think of anything else since she used her safe word and walked out of my house—out of my life. I'd finally given up and gone into the office to try to work my way through my feelings. It wasn't helping.

"Talk to me, man." He leaned forward in the chair, concern etched on his face.

"No. Not yet," I added to soften my words. He cared about me. I appreciated that, even if I didn't want to share what happened with Alex. I was ashamed, and I needed to hold onto those feelings on my own for a while longer.

"You really like her." His eyebrows hit his hairline, shock clear on his face.

Like was an understatement. After she walked out my door, taking her light and laughter and leaving me behind, I realized my feelings for Alex were a lot stronger than *like*. I loved her and instead of telling her, I offered her money to let me fuck her. There was no way in hell I was coming back from that. If I were her, I wouldn't talk to me again.

I couldn't imagine never talking to her again, never holding her. The sex was phenomenal. There weren't enough words in my vocabulary to describe it, but it was my soul that ached for her. I'd spent the better part of a day and night trying to convince my stupid heart I'd survive her leaving. I knew now I wouldn't. What I didn't know was what the fuck to do about it.

"It's more than that, isn't it?" Jared asked when I didn't respond.

I nodded, unwilling or unable to say the words. At this point, who the fuck cared? I was wrecked either way. I'd hurt Alex so badly she had to use her safe word to protect herself. *From me.* With a few careless words, I'd managed to do what I couldn't do with a crop or flogger or whip.

"You go after everything you want, and I've never seen you miss." He held up his hand before I could protest. "Julie didn't count. You didn't really want *her*. You wanted what you thought she could be. That was never going to be the relationship you wanted it to be."

"It's complicated."

"It always is, man."

"Excuse me, Mr. Jensen," my assistant cut in on the intercom. "I've got an Elena Patrick on the line. She's insisting she speak with you about a home tour."

I paused for a moment, the kernel of an idea forming. I couldn't undo the damage I'd done, but maybe there was a way for me to avoid being an ass moving forward.

"Find me if you want to talk," Jared said on his way out the door.

I nodded, grateful even though we both knew I had no intention of taking him up on his offer.

"Put her through."

MONDAYS SUCKED UNDER the best of circumstances, but it wouldn't matter what day of the week it was. Nothing felt right since I used my safe word and walked out of Erik's house.

I still couldn't believe I let myself get in so deep. I knew better. And I couldn't even get mad at him for the way he'd propositioned me because he was playing by the ground rules we'd established. I was the dumbass who'd gone and fallen in love, which meant his offer of money for time wasn't a clean exchange anymore. It broke my heart. My stupid, over-involved, what the fuck was I thinking heart.

I had no illusions about what happened next. I went back to my life, and he went back to his, the way we'd always planned to. I had no illusions of Jensen riding down the street, his head poking through the sunroof of his stretch limo, waiting to climb my fire escape to true love and happily ever after. This wasn't *Pretty Woman* or some other Pygmalion knock-off.

The thing that bugged me even more was that I had to remind myself that I didn't need Jensen to save me. That had never been our thing. I was a woman in my full power. I had been before I met Jensen, and I would be again. It might take a fair bit of alcohol and a tear-soaked binge watch of the first two seasons of *Outlander*, but eventually I'd bounce back.

I was going to start by sharing the pain au chocolat I'd picked up at the corner bakery with Charlotte and then

I was going to find out how long it would take to get my life back to normal. And I was going to ignore like the queen of denial the fact that things would never be the same as they were. It was the classic *fake it 'til you make it* technique and I planned to work it like a rock star.

"I come bearing gifts," I said, rapping on Charlotte's open door and holding the sack of pastries and the to-go cups of coffee out in front of me like the toll for entrance.

"I love you. Get in here." Charlotte snagged the bag of pastries and one of the cups of coffee from my hand, leaving me standing in the doorway in clear demonstration of her priorities. "You are a lifesaver. I haven't had time for breakfast and I'm starving."

"I aim to please." I collapsed on the sofa, taking a swallow of coffee and praying it didn't take too long for the caffeine to kick in. Sleep had been hard to come by what with all the weeping and such. "You said you've got news?"

"I do," she said around a mouthful of pastry. "The movie company dropped the suit. It's over."

"It's over? What does it mean? How much do I have to pay them?" My chest tightened, not in anticipation, but I wasn't going to look closer at my feelings. *Denial. It's a thing.*

"Nothing. I got them to agree to settle for a simple name change."

She looked so proud of herself. The last thing I wanted was to be ungrateful, but the idea of rebranding myself felt overwhelming. Exhausting.

"You can't do business as the Gentleman's Submissive anymore, but the Gentlemen's Submissive is just fine. One letter—*a* to *e*—and you're done."

I couldn't ignore the irony in going from singular to plural, not when that's exactly what happened in my personal life.

"This feels anticlimactic," she said, licking the chocolate off her fingers. "I expected you to be more excited about this."

"I am. Honestly." I reached over to touch her hand and snagged the bag with the pastry. I wasn't going to be able to deal with the emotions threatening to swamp me without some serious help. Chocolate was a start, at least. "Thank you."

"Nu-uh." She pinned me with her gaze and shook her head. "Something else is going on. It's that attorney, isn't it? Did he do something? He's already on shaky ground with his firm. Say the word and I'll make it shakier."

"No, it's nothing like that. Things with him just didn't work out the way I thought they would."

"I'm sorry," she said, concern etched on her face. "What can I do?"

It was the reason I hadn't told her over the weekend. Charlotte was a fixer. It was her superpower. She'd want to help me fix things with Erik and when she realized she couldn't, she'd try to convince me ending things was for the best. I wasn't ready for any of that.

"Nothing. It's fine." It wasn't, but with fourteen or so hours of Scottish time travel and a fifth of whiskey, I'd be able to fake it. "What about you?" I asked, finally pulling out of my self-absorbed stupor enough to notice the smudges under her eyes she'd used very expensive concealer to try to hide. "Did you get things sorted with your old friend?"

I swallowed on the word *friend*. One more thing that would be forever connected to Jensen, and I was going to have to call Elena and tell her the house fell through. *Fuck*.

"Actually, yes. That case is settled too. Jack and his wife are reconciling. Turns out the partner set my client up to try to get controlling share of the company." She ran a hand over her already smooth hair, her lips curving in an uncomfortable smile.

"Are you okay? I know you really liked him." It looked like both of us were nursing broken hearts.

"A marriage is still intact. I have to be happy about that, right?"

"On an intellectual level, yeah, but it can still suck too."

"It does."

We sat for a moment in mutual malaise, consoling ourselves with chocolate and coffee. It was an okay short-term fix but led to ass spreading problems long-term. We needed a better plan.

"Let's get everyone together for dinner and drinks, heavy on the drinks."

"I'd love that, but it has to be tomorrow. I've got a work thing tonight."

"Tomorrow then. I'll set it up." I had plans, things to do, reasons to move forward, even if it was just drinking with my girlfriends. Forward movement counted. "Call me if you need me." I gave her hand a squeeze and stood, feeling better because I'd taken the focus off myself.

"Same goes for you."

The good feeling lasted the length of the elevator ride. By the time I hit the muggy heat of the street, the sadness and sense of loss was back in full force. I thumbed open my phone and dialed Elena's number. *May as well get all the shitty things out of the way at once rather than spread out the misery.*

"Alex! I'm so glad you called." She squealed through the other end of the line and I moved the phone a couple inches away from my ear to save what was left of my hearing. "I have so many things to tell you."

"I've got something to tell you too."

"Me first," she said, practically gasping for breath. "I know you said you'd work things out with him…"

"Elena, wait."

"But I couldn't help myself," she said, talking over my warning. "I just got off the phone with your Erik and he said yes!"

"He said yes?" *That couldn't be right.* She had to have misunderstood him. Jensen hadn't wanted his house included on the tour. There was no way he'd say yes after everything that happened. "To the house tour?"

"I think his exact words were 'It would be my pleasure to do anything Alex asks of me.' He said it in that deep voice of his. Kind of gave me butterflies."

I knew the voice. It was the one that washed over me like melted caramel. The one that ordered me to stay still and then set about trying to make me squirm. The one I never thought I'd hear again pitched low against my ear while its owner's hands did delicious things to my body.

I ended the call more confused than I'd been when I started the day. There was absolutely no good reason for Erik to say yes to the home tour and a dozen reasons for him to say no. Before I could twist my thoughts into too tight of a pretzel, my phone rang again. Peter's number flashed on my screen and my stomach dropped so fast, I almost missed a step.

"This is Lexi." The old greeting felt awkward and wrong. It had only been a couple of weeks since I used it, but slipping into the old cadence felt like relearning a foreign language. "How can I help you, Peter?"

"I was wondering if I could book another session. Things with Sarah went so well after last time. We've got an anniversary coming up and I want to blow her mind. There's a book she's been reading and I'm not sure how to do some of the things in it."

"I was actually on my way to the studio. I've got an unexpected opening in my schedule if you have time now?"

"Fantastic."

The enthusiasm in his voice was an inverse proportion of my own feelings but that was just too damn bad. I had a business to resurrect.

ERIK

I WIPED MY hands on my slacks as I waited for the elevator to arrive. I figured I had one chance to fix my fuck-up—if that—and I had no intention of blowing it. I'd do whatever it took to get Alex back in my life, even if it meant finding a way to be comfortable with her work. I hadn't worked out all the hows but I wasn't conflicted about the what. I wanted Alex in my arms, in my bed, in my life, and I was willing to move heaven and earth to get it. I loved her. I'd tell her over and over again every day until she believed me and was ready to love me back.

I hadn't let myself consider that she might never get to that point. I was rolling forward full steam ahead with the *failure is not an option* plan. I was still nervous as shit, which was where the sweaty palms came in. I managed to push the elevator call button without leaving a sweat-streaked smudge behind as I rode to Alex's studio. She wasn't at her apartment and a surprisingly helpful Charlotte hadn't known where she was but she mentioned removing the cease-and-desist, which meant there was every likelihood that Alex had gone back to work. That's what I was banking on and since her phone went right to voicemail, it seemed like a safe bet.

I planned to knock on the door and throw myself at her mercy for a change, and if she wasn't there or if she was with a client, well then, I'd wait. The idea of her with someone else twisted something in my gut but she was worth it. I couldn't love her and expect her to change who she was or give up what she'd built because it made me uncomfortable. I was man enough to deal with her work.

I rapped on the door and waited, ready to prostrate myself at the first sign of her softening. I waited for so long; I'd almost given up by the time the door opened and she stood in front of me, wearing yoga pants and my Tulane shirt she'd taken with her when she left me. Seeing her in my clothes hit every one of my possessive buttons and then I noticed the red rims around her eyes and my heart broke all over again. *She'd been crying, and it was my fucking fault.*

"Why are you here?" She squared her shoulders like she was steeling herself against something—against me—but she shifted her body just enough to let me enter.

"First to tell you I'm sorry." I'd worked out the order on the ride over. *Apology first, then declaration of undying love.*

"For what? You were just doing what we agreed to," she said, crossing her arms over her chest. She couldn't be more unavailable to me if she was wrapped in chains and padlocked. But she wasn't mostly naked with a client, so I'd take my wins where I could get them.

"I made a mistake. I never should have made you that offer."

"I don't understand. You just offered to extend what we were already doing."

This apology thing wasn't going the way I'd pictured it. I looked at the set of her jaw and saw the whole thing heading south fast.

"I love you. I should have told you right away instead of trying to get you to quit your business. I don't know how to make any of this work out, but Alex, I want to try."

"What?" Her eyes were the size of saucers, but she'd relaxed her grip on herself, which had to be a positive sign.

"The client thing. I'm not normally jealous. I'll try to find a way to compartmentalize so I can deal with your work. You've built a business that's important to you. It's not fair for me to expect you to give it up." I'd started out wanting to ruin her. It was kind of funny how things worked out sometimes.

"I meant the other thing. The love thing."

"Oh," I said, not bothering to try to hide my smile. "I love you like crazy. I want to fall asleep with you in my arms every night and wake up with you every morning. I understand if you're not there yet. I can be patient." It would be hard as hell, but even saying the words aloud eased the tension I'd been carrying in my chest the past couple of days. Alex was worth waiting for.

"I love you too."

I didn't give her a chance to take the words back or qualify them. I closed the distance between us in two strides and scooped her up in my arms, kissing her until the ache in my heart started to wane, replaced with something warmer. Hotter.

I tunneled my hands into her hair, anchoring her in place for my mouth. She met me with a hunger of her own, her tongue finding mine, tasting and teasing as we breathed each other in.

"We'll figure out the work thing. I promise," I said when I managed to break the kiss. I wanted to take her right there on the floor, to slide inside her and claim her, but I needed her to know I wouldn't try to change her. That I loved her exactly the way she was—job and all.

"I'm closing the Gentleman's Submissive. I don't want to do it anymore."

"Why? Not for me?" I couldn't take it if she grew to resent me for taking her away from something she loved.

"Not entirely." She searched my face with her gaze and I found myself getting distracted by the look in her eyes. A look I'd gotten glimpses of but hadn't recognized before. *Love.*

"I had a client scheduled for this afternoon. For now, actually, but I couldn't go through with it. After what we did together, anything other than genuine surrender made me feel like a fake. And I didn't want to surrender to anyone but you. You see my dilemma."

"I do."

"I thought I might skip the academic thing and go straight to writing my book. It's what I wanted to do from the beginning and I've got enough money saved to give it a try for a couple of months. If I can't sell it, I'll figure something else out."

"You'll sell it," I said, as sure of her success as I was of things like gravity. The woman I loved was beautiful and brilliant and had a unique way of looking at the world. I had no doubt she'd master whatever she turned her attention to as easily as she'd mastered me.

"I don't have to figure it out now." She linked her fingers with mine and brought our joined hands to her lips. "I was planning on salving my broken heart with *Outlander* reruns and Scotch. We could go home and I could read to you instead."

I fucking loved the way it sounded when she said home.

"We do it naked, and you try not to come while I do my best to make you."

"Is that a dare?" she asked, her eyes shining mischievously.

"Absolutely." I wrapped my arms around her, fitting her body to mine and feeling at home for the first time since she'd walked out my door.

"Deal," she whispered the second before her lips met mine and the world dissolved into Alex and me and the love we'd make together.

Epilogue

I LISTENED TO THE WOMAN with the dark hair hammer away on the keys of her laptop. She was there every day, in the same seat, pounding away at something. I'd started to believe I was imagining her because she almost never talked to anyone and rarely did more than type and stare off into space. She seemed so wrapped up in her own little world I'd wondered if I'd created her from mine, but then the guy in the suit showed up and everything changed. Her face lit up, softening. Focusing. He kissed her and they looked at each other with so much—it had to be love, nothing else was that big—I knew they were real. I couldn't make those feelings up. I didn't have the frame of reference.

Besides, I hadn't had a hallucination in years. Or maybe I had. I couldn't be sure. The city wore its crazy out on the surface for everyone to see. It's one of the reasons I'd chosen it. With the ghost tours, voodoo shops, and tourists abandoning normal society limits in favor of the excesses of Bourbon St. and the French Quarter, day-to-day life in New Orleans was weirder than anything my off-kilter brain made up. Or maybe not, but it was close enough to make the city a comfortable fit for me.

"Can I get a macchiato, please? Whole milk, not skim."

I heard the voice over the clacking of the keyboard and the ambient coffee shop noise. Its lyrical melody played over the sound of the barista foaming milk and the couple two tables over arguing about whether they could afford a new sofa before someone's "shrew of a mother" came for Thanksgiving. It was as if I wore one of those hearing aids that isolated sounds, tuned to the specific frequency of that voice.

Careful not to knock my coffee onto my notes, I turned in the direction of the sound. I wasn't sure what I'd been expecting but it wasn't her.

She was perfect. Red hair with the barest dusting of freckles over her slender nose with a jawline strong enough for a Celtic princess. She looked like she'd be at home in the Scottish Highlands or painted with woad and dancing with the Druids in the shadow of the standing stones. She was tall and willowy, and everything I'd ever imagined in a woman. *Perfect.*

So perfect, in fact, I started to question if my brain had created her to ease an ache I hadn't realized I felt. I'd gotten so used to being alone; I stopped feeling lonely a long time ago. Until I heard her voice and a cavern opened up inside me so deep I was scared to move for fear of being swallowed whole.

I froze in place, watching as she took her coffee, smiled at the barista and crossed the room to the dark-haired woman. She brushed past my table, close enough that I had to clench my hands into fists to keep from reaching out to touch her. I sucked in my breath and inhaled the sweet scent of toasted sugar and butter surrounding her like her own special perfume.

The women greeted each other like they'd been friends forever. Breaking one of my own rules of behavior, I strained to listen to their conversation. They talked about proposals, and agents and publishing contracts. And then they talked about the man in the suit. Erik—he had a name now; but I didn't need to hear his name to know who they meant—the dark-haired woman loved him and he loved her. He was the only person who fit. He'd given her a ring and they needed a cake from her friend.

Meredith.

She had a name, and I had a reason to turn away. To forget I'd ever seen her. To try to bury the loneliness before it ate away at the tenuous peace I'd built for myself. Because I was broken—a monster—and a woman who smelled like cookies didn't belong with a wolf.

Dear Reader,

I hope you enjoyed a Deposition and a Dare. My author friends knew it as my shiny ball because it's the story that's been distracting me for years until I finally broke down and wrote it. I love Alex. She says the things I sometimes think and has a kind of arrogance combined with Saint Bernard puppy eagerness I can relate to (It's the puppy awkwardness thing not the arrogance. Maybe. Or not. Don't ask my family.)

Obviously, Meredith's story is the next book in the Saints and Sinners series. She and her Wolf are woven deep in my heart. I love the idea of a damaged but spectacular hero and a woman strong enough to see the truth and beauty of him. The link for my mailing list is below. Sign up and you'll be the first to know when their story is available.

I'd love to hear from you at authorevelynadams@gmail.com and you can sign up for juicy bits and find out about new releases at www.authorevelynadams.com I hope to talk to you soon!

Many Blessings!
Evelyn